CAST OF CHARACTERS

In Emerald Cove, blood is thicker than water.

Seth Evans—An explosion leaves him stranded with his lovely assistant, but will he survive with his heart intact?

Emma Carpenter—She appears shy and unassuming, but is there more to this assistant than meets the eye?

Marcus Evans—One of the recently discovered genetically engineered superhumans, the U.S. Navy SEAL will do anything to protect his adopted family.

Drew Evans—Seth's cousin left the navy after a failed rescue attempt, but he still feels a duty to help those in need....

About the Author

There aren't many things **Vickie Taylor** likes better than a few hours of precious quiet time and a spine-tingling, page-turning romantic suspense novel. She loves the excitement, the danger, the intrigue and of course, the passionate drama of the romance unfolding against all odds. Knowing this about her, it's no surprise then that Vickie was ecstatic at being asked to participate in the FAMILY SECRETS continuity series.

"The FAMILY SECRETS books are exactly the kind of stories I like to read—and write. They're edgy, suspenseful and full of twists and turns. The characters are smart and sexy, yet layered with real personalities and conflicts," Vickie says. "It was truly an honor to work with such a great group of authors to bring this series to life."

Vickie lives in a small town in Texas with a menagerie of horses, dogs and cats. Please visit her Web site at: www.VickieTaylor.com.

RIPPLE
EFFECT

VICKIE
TAYLOR

Published by Silhouette Books
America's Publisher of Contemporary Romance

Special thanks and acknowledgment are given to Vickie Taylor for her contribution to the FAMILY SECRETS series.

 SILHOUETTE BOOKS

ISBN 0-373-61380-6

RIPPLE EFFECT

Visit us at www.silhouettefamilysecrets.com

Printed in U.S.A.

FAMILY SECRETS

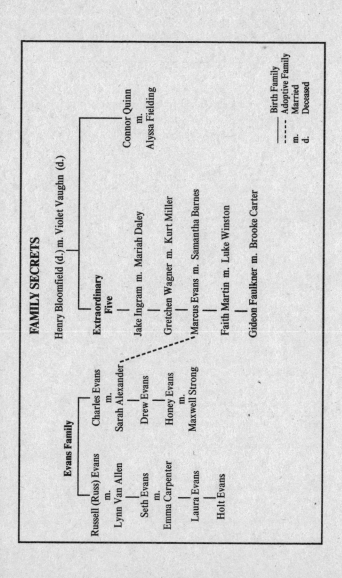

Henry Bloomfield (d.) m. Violet Vaughn (d.)

Connor Quinn
m.
Alyssa Fielding

Extraordinary Five

Jake Ingram m. Mariah Daley

Gretchen Wagner m. Kurt Miller

Marcus Evans m. Samantha Barnes

Faith Martin m. Luke Winston

Gideon Faulkner m. Brooke Carter

Evans Family

Russell (Russ) Evans
m.
Lynn Van Allen

Charles Evans
m.
Sarah Alexander

Seth Evans
m.
Emma Carpenter

Drew Evans

Honey Evans
m.
Maxwell Strong

Laura Evans

Holt Evans

——— Birth Family
----- Adoptive Family
m. Married
d. Deceased

One

*A*gent Omega clutched the bulky laundry bag tighter against her pounding heart. Dark glasses hid her furtive glances up and down Pompano Boulevard as she melted into the pedestrian flow. Her alarm watch had yet to chime 8:00 a.m., but already Emerald Cove, one of the Florida Keys' smallest but most popular vacation spots, hummed with activity. Beach lovers and fishermen spilled from their hotels and headed toward the waterfront under a dazzling early June sun. Women wearing shorts and sandals window-shopped along blocks of sparkling glass storefronts. Businessmen swam through the meandering crowd determinedly, cell phones pressed to their ears.

Just another day in paradise.

Agent Omega shuffled along the sidewalk with the civilians, her senses on high alert.

Delivery was scheduled for oh-eight-hundred. Any member of the milieu on the street could have been watching her. The businessman seemingly absorbed in the morning headlines as he waited at the bus stop. Was that a bulge in the armpit of his jacket, or merely a poorly cut suit? The gray-haired tourist with her floppy straw hat and a beach bag big enough to hide a howitzer. The young mother pushing a stroller.

Any one of them could have been sent to intercept her.

Any one of them could have been the enemy.

A bead of sweat rolled between her breasts as the plain manila envelope tucked inside the laundry bag crinkled reassuringly against her chest. She was almost there. This Friday, as every Friday, she would deliver her package on time.

The Do Not Walk sign at the corner ahead flashed its amber warning. She hung back, forcing anyone who might be tailing her to pass or risk exposing himself. On the outside, she was as calm as a placid summer sea. Beneath the surface, a riptide of adrenaline coursed through her.

God, she loved this spy stuff.

The light changed. A quick dash across the street and she'd be safely at the rendezvous. Pulling in a victorious breath, Agent Omega stepped off the curb—

Emma Carpenter never saw the attack coming. A blur of electric yellow and vivid purple clipped her shoulder, knocking her out of her daydream, through this reality and nearly into the next. As if in slow motion, the laundry bag sailed out of her grasp. Blouses poofed out. Unmentionables wafted in the sky like lace clouds. The manila folder hidden within the clothes arced through the air above her head.

Drowning out the drone of traffic, the blaring horns, the vendor hawking sunscreen and beach umbrellas on the corner, Emma's heartbeat thrummed in her ears.

Lud-dub. Lud-dub.

She wobbled on her sensible pumps. Her arms flailed. Laundry flew every which way, but it was the envelope that held Emma's rapt attention. The package fluttered on a breeze heavy with the scent of brine and turned over once on its slow descent. Sunshine glittered off its metal clasp.

Lud-dub. Lud-dub.

Still off balance, she lurched for the packet she was supposed to deliver to the dry cleaner's across the street. She willed an extra inch to the length of her arm. Prayed for another millimeter of fingertip.

And hit the hot pavement with an audible "Ooff!" as she watched her precious envelope hit the curb and slither into the sewer just beyond her reach.

Her watch chirped its 8:00 a.m. warning. Time to deliver her package.

Lud-dub.

"Hey, lady, are you okay?"

Groaning, Emma slapped her hand over her watch to silence the alarm, then cautiously lifted her head. A boy in a bright yellow tank top and purple bicycle helmet kicked his skateboard into the air, caught it and tucked it under his arm in one smooth move. "Geez, I'm sorry. I didn' mean ta hit ya. But you were walking kind of slow-like."

Because she'd been daydreaming again, Emma realized. Agent Omega... Ha! Some secret agent she made. Taken out by a Tango that had yet to reach puberty.

Not to mention losing her package.

She stared into the dark mouth of the sewer. The faint gurgle of water whispered out of the darkness. What was she going to tell Yankovich?

"You're not hurt or anythin', are you?" the kid who'd hit her asked, chewing on his thumbnail.

Noticing that she was drawing a crowd, lying sprawled half on the sidewalk, half on the street,

Emma sighed gustily and pushed herself to her hands and knees. "No, I'm not hurt."

One by one, the bystanders drifted away. She brushed off the pebbles embedded in her knees and found two gigantic holes in her panty hose. "Great. Just great," she muttered, gently tugging the nylon up to minimize the exposure and succeeding only in sending a half a dozen runs ripping down to her ankles.

"You're not gonna, like, report this or anything, are you? 'Cuz I already got fined once for riding on the sidewalks."

"No, I'm not going to report this." Emma straightened and looked into the sandy-haired boy's earnest blue eyes. Eleven, she guessed. Maybe twelve years old. He was going to be a heartbreaker by the time he hit high school. It wouldn't do to let him start charming his way out of trouble too early.

She propped her fists on her hips. "If you help me clean up this mess, that is."

"Sure. Whatever." The boy bent to pick up a bra, but froze midreach. His cheeks flamed. He sputtered a moment, gaze darting everywhere but at the garment in front of him. Finally his eyes shifted toward the gutter and lit on an alternative to collecting women's underwear. "Uh, your papers went down the drain. I could get them for you. There's a loose manhole cover over on Grove Street."

Emma thought about it. For about half a second. "It's not safe to go crawling around the sewer."

The boy's back went ramrod straight, as if she'd accused him of being a yellow-belly. "I could do it."

"I'm sure you could. But I'm not having you get swept out to sea on my account."

Yankovich's blustery face caught her attention from

the sidewalk in front of the dry cleaner's across the street. He scowled at her. Pretending she hadn't seen him, she waved the boy away. "Now scram, before I change my mind about reporting this. And call the city about that manhole cover," she called after him.

When he was gone she scooped up the rest of her clothes, ramming them into her sack and cinching it tightly. Nothing like turning on the bilge pumps after the boat's sunk, she thought morosely, and crossed the street to face her contact without the goods she'd come to deliver.

"What the hell happened out there, Carpenter?" Yankovich growled around the cigar clamped between his teeth.

"Nothing, sir. Just a minor accident." She followed him into Dun Right Laundry and Dry Cleaning.

"Where's your report?"

Emma dumped her laundry bag on the counter as she did each Friday morning at eight o'clock. Only this time the report that she usually handed over to Yankovich with her dirty clothes wasn't in the bag. She braced her shoulders. "It's in the sewer, sir."

Yankovich took the cigar from his mouth so he could snarl at her better. A thin ribbon of smoke curled in two points above his head, like devil's horns. "Well, hell's bells. What's it doing in the damn sewer?"

Emma jolted slightly as he punctuated each word with a jab of his cigar into the air. "I dropped it, sir."

"Oh, that's just fine," he said, smiling like a barracuda. "You dropped highly sensitive documents into the sewer."

"Yes, sir." Emma swallowed. Silence loomed large around her as Yankovich dragged deep on his stogie.

"I'll get it back," she said, her mouth running quicker than her brain, as it sometimes did. "There's a loose manhole cover over on Grove Street—"

"For God's sake you're not going to go crawling around a storm drain," he bellowed. The tinkling of the bell over the door behind Emma quieted him. He practically snatched the claim ticket out of the woman's hand. Moments later, he returned with a few pairs of pressed slacks and a plain button-down shirt covered in plastic. When the woman was gone, he picked up Emma's bag for show.

"Yer a secretary, for God's sake," he hissed in a voice more suited to secrecy. "Least you're supposed to be. You can't go skulking around in the sewers. What if someone saw you?"

"But my report—"

"What was in it?"

"A list of appointments my client took this week." Yankovich would know that *client* referred to her mark. Her target. The man she'd been sent to spy on. Her heart gave a little thump. She was really a spy. Finally. Rallying around that thought, she lifted her chin and continued. "His calendar for next week. Incoming and outgoing phone calls. The usual."

"Nothing, in other words." Reproach gleamed in Yankovich's black eyes.

The skin at the back of Emma's neck prickled. She didn't like being bullied. Even by her boss. "It would help if I knew what you were looking for."

"Exchanges of large sums of money, clandestine meetings, contacts from outside the U.S.—say Rebelia or Holzberg, for example."

Frustration boiled in Emma. She'd been undercover at her *client's* company for nearly six months now, filing and fetching for him while posing as his secretary. If there was anything illicit going on at Evans Yachts, it was beyond her ability to find it.

"My client sells very expensive boats. Exchanges of large sums of money are a daily occurrence. He's a busy man who doesn't like distractions, so his meetings are almost always held in private. And his clients—legitimate clients—come from all over the world. Including Rebelia and Holzberg."

Yankovich leaned across the counter. The stench of his cigar made Emma's eyes water.

"You're not digging deep enough," he said, his black eyes empty and hard as onyx. She wondered how long he'd been in this business. Long enough to lose his soul, she guessed. "You've got to get closer to the project. Closer to *him*."

The emphasis on *him* sent an electric ripple over Emma's skin. Seth Evans, CEO of Evans Yachts, Emerald Cove's most eligible bachelor, entrepreneur and…enigma.

Surely Yankovich wasn't suggesting she get closer to Seth in a sexual sense. Better women than she had tried to get close to him. Rich women. Successful women. Beautiful, sophisticated women. None stayed on his plate for long, though not for lack of trying.

As his secretary, she'd seen how he operated. He humored them a while—and took care of some of his own needs as he did so, she assumed—then let them down easy. It wasn't that he was a cruel man. Quite the opposite. He was just…closed. Work was his only obsession. Nothing—no one—else got under his skin.

Least of all, her.

She doubted he even realized the effect he had on women. Lord knew, she did her best to hide it. He was

way out of her league. She was much more likely to
gain his confidence as his trusty girl Friday than his
lover.

And she should *not* be disappointed in that fact.

"Maybe there isn't anything to find," she said, as
much to make herself feel better as to placate Yankovich. "Maybe he is exactly what he appears—a hard-
working, honest businessman trying to make a buck
and build a company."

"Everybody's got a little dirt under their nails if
you look hard enough. I want to know how deep your
client's runs, that's all. I want to know about anything
in his past or present that could be used against him.
I want to know if he's got a weakness. Something that
could be exploited."

"I thought our mission here was—"

Yankovich snared her wrist with his meaty hand and
pulled her close, silencing her. His gaze darted around
the dry cleaning shop nervously, as if an eavesdropper
might materialize out of thin air, then settled on her
like an iron collar. "That laundry will be ready Monday after five."

Suppressing a shudder at the depth of the menace
in Yankovich's glare, she nodded, realizing her mistake. She should've known better than to discuss the
nature of her mission in a public place.

Guess she still had a lot to learn about the spy business.

His eyes narrowed before he let her go. "You run
along to work now. You got a job to do. You don't
do it, you might be looking for another one soon."

The thinly veiled threat jabbed Emma like a poker
in the ribs. It wasn't Seth Evans she had to worry
about firing her.

She yanked her wrist out of Yankovich's clasp. "If you know someone more qualified for the job, you're welcome to have them apply."

Over her dead body.

She'd worked hard to earn this job, but it was a one-time shot. Either she proved herself here, and by doing so earned the respect of her superiors, or she failed, and resigned herself to a life of menial labor for real, not just as a cover story.

No way was she going to let the latter happen. She'd had enough tedium for one lifetime. She wanted some excitement in her life. She was going somewhere.

But right now, she thought as she stepped back onto the sidewalk in front of the dry cleaners, she was going to work.

And this time she wasn't leaving until she knew all there was to know about Seth Evans.

"Yeah, Pop, I know." Seth Evans cocked his shoulder to hold the phone against his ear. Shoving aside a file folder, he raised his feet to the mahogany desk he'd inherited when he'd taken over the helm of Evans Yachts from his dad three years ago. Ordinarily he frowned on such unprofessional posture, but Seth was alone in the office this morning. Besides, there were some perks to being CEO.

"The regatta is just three months away, son. Your brother is getting anxious."

Seth stretched to work the kinks out of his neck, and smiled. "Tell Holt to furl his sails, Pop. I'll have his new girlfriend ready for their first date soon."

Evans Yachts built—and raced—some of the fastest boats on the water. Seth built them; his little brother, Holt, raced them. This year the company was introducing a new model, lighter, faster, more maneuverable than ever. Or so they hoped.

Holt had been whining for a month about wanting to take the new boat, *The Unicorn,* out for a sea trial. With his usual entourage of nubile, bikini-clad, yacht-racing groupies in tow, of course.

Not that any of them had a chance with Holt. Seth's little brother's first love—maybe his only love—was a fast boat.

On the other end of the phone line, his father chuckled. "Holt says to tell you that at least he *has* a girl-friend."

"Hardee-har."

Let Holt have the fast boats. The races. The glory.

Seth had a mistress just as exciting.

The business.

Since he'd first set foot in his father's plush office, he'd been enchanted by the subtle manipulation of numbers that made the difference between profit and loss. The challenge of the balance sheet. The thrill of a healthy financial statement. Like any good lover, the business kept him on his toes, never let him get too comfortable.

And he was faithful to her.

When his father spoke again, his voice was lower, serious. "Holt's boat isn't what I'm worried about, son."

Tension formed a knot in Seth's chest. He lowered his voice. "We're making good progress on the project, Dad. The electromagnetic hull-plating Gideon designed for the Stingray is holding up well in testing. Looks like it's impervious to both sonar and radar, just like he said it would be."

Thank the stars for that. And for Gideon Faulkner.

Some people might not have taken a risk on hiring a man with Gideon's history for a project as sensitive as designing a new stealth submarine for the U.S. Navy. After all, the man had engineered the greatest bank heist of all time.

Seth still had trouble reconciling the almost painfully shy, sheltered-to-the-point-of-being-naive young man he'd hired with the Gideon Faulkner, code name Achilles, accused of jeopardizing the entire world economy by engineering the World Bank heist, in which 350 billion dollars had been electronically transferred into untraceable accounts around the globe.

Seth shook his head. The story was almost too fantastic to believe, yet by all accounts, true.

Gideon was the product of Code Proteus—one of the first experiments in human genetic engineering. The brainchild of Dr. Henry Bloomfield, Gideon and each of his five siblings received special DNA, preprogrammed with unique specialties. Gideon's gift was the ability to comprehend and create technology.

That gift for technology made Gideon invaluable to Seth.

And to the nasty coalition that had brainwashed Gideon since childhood and used him to commit the World Bank heist.

If it hadn't been for Gideon's brothers and sisters, reunited by the eldest sibling, Jake, after being secretly adopted into separate homes for their own protection, Gideon might still be held prisoner by the Coalition, forced to do their dirty work.

But thanks to the "Extraordinary Five," as they'd been dubbed before a sixth sibling had been discovered, the Coalition had been destroyed and Gideon freed. The genetically engineered children, especially Jake Ingram, were being hailed as heroes.

Now it was time for Gideon to find his own place in life—a place he and his new wife, Brooke, chose of their own free will. A place where they could raise the baby they were expecting in peace.

Seth was just grateful they'd chosen Emerald Cove. He supposed he had his meathead cousin Marcus to thank for that. It was Marcus who had convinced his brother Gideon to join Evans Yachts and Project Stingray.

Talk about unbelievable—Marcus, the adopted cousin he so often accused of having more muscles than brains, was Gideon's brother, one of the Extraordinary Six. Turned out he hadn't come by all those muscles by accident, but by design.

Genetic design.

Marcus's gift from Dr. Bloomfield was strength.

Seth grinned to himself. At least now he had an excuse for all those fights he'd lost to Marcus as a kid.

"What about speed?" his father asked, drawing Seth back to their discussion of the submarine.

Seth tapped a pencil on his desk blotter, a narrow pang stabbing his chest. "Computer projections put her within three and a half knots of navy specs."

"Then you're three and a half knots shy."

"I'm working on it." The pang in his chest grew tendrils, reached up into his head and started to throb. He'd taken a big chance, breaking into a whole new field with this navy contract. The company's reputation—not to mention a whole lot of money—rode on Stingray's success.

Then there was the matter of national security. Stingray was to be used as an insertion vehicle for rapid deployment of Navy SEALs into hostile territories. It was touted as America's newest weapon against terrorism. Having lost a Harvard buddy in the World Trade Center a few years back, Seth drew more than a little satisfaction from his contribution to Homeland Security.

Or he would, if he could squeeze another four nautical miles per hour out of an already overworked engine design.

For the first time, Seth wondered if he and his father had bitten off more than they could chew with the Stingray project. They were simple pleasure boat builders, after all. Even if they were known worldwide for their unique keel designs, and for utilizing the latest polymers to make a lighter, faster vessel. They were already nearly two years and several million dollars into this project. If they failed, a lot of people were going to be disappointed. Starting with him.

His father cleared his throat. "What about Gideon? Has he looked at the plans?"

Seth pinched the bridge of his nose against the building headache. "This is more of a mechanical problem than a technological one, Pop. Not really Gideon's specialty. But yeah, he looked. The problem is, to get more power we have to make the engine bigger."

"And when you make the engine bigger, you also make it louder."

"Right. Even Gideon's whiz-bang hull plating can't cover up that much noise. It makes the sub vulnerable."

"The navy brass is expecting to see a prototype in three months, Seth."

"Three months and twenty-six days, actually." The

last week of September, during the regatta, which would provide the perfect cover for a bunch of old Salts to visit Emerald Cove without arousing suspicion. "Did the admiral send over the updated weapons systems schematics?"

The chime over the elevator doors that opened into Seth's sixth-floor suite sounded, and he watched as his secretary, Emma Carpenter, blew into the outer office like a tropical storm. His abdomen tightened against the inevitable stirring in his gut that came each morning with his first glimpse of her. The physical reaction to his usually quiet, unassuming assistant was a continual source of both annoyance and puzzlement to him.

She really wasn't his type. When he'd hired her, he'd made it clear that he expected a level of professionalism in his office, and she'd complied to the extreme. Her boxy-cut suit jackets, high-collared cotton blouses and knee-length skirts could hardly be called provocative. Yet when Seth looked at her, all he could see was the smooth curve of her bust—plentiful without being disproportionate to her stature—her tight waist, trim calves and slender ankles.

The tight knot of wavy auburn hair she wore at the base of her skull inspired Seth to fantasize about how that kinky mass of curls would look set free. How they would feel tangled around his fists. Even her makeup was understated, but instead of detracting from her appearance, the lack of cover only highlighted the natural arc of her cheekbones.

Without even trying, she was a constant source of distraction to him. He didn't understand it. Didn't much like it, either.

He had too damned much work to do to be lusting

after his secretary. Not that that stopped him. His libido didn't seem to care that he had a submarine to build.

Seth's father said something about missile system designs that would have to be integrated with something. He wasn't sure what. He was more intrigued with Emma. It wasn't often he got the chance to sit back and appreciate her unawares.

Normally she moved through the office like a wraith. He'd turn and find her behind him at the oddest moments without having heard her approach. Or look up from a phone call to find her at his door without having seen her move from her own desk.

But today was definitely not a normal day.

She locked her purse in her desk, then stalked to the coffeemaker where she filled a clean mug from the overhead cabinet. She bustled toward his office.

Seth noticed she seemed to be listing to port, wobbling as if she'd hurt herself, or broken a heel on one of those conservative pumps she wore. There was nothing in the world he should have found appealing about those granny shoes, and yet every time he looked at them, he smiled, thinking how much he'd like to take them off her.

He forced his gaze away from her feet, found himself just as lost in her face. Half a dozen tendrils of hair had come loose from her bun and flew wildly about her head. A swipe of grease smudged one of her classic cheeks.

She stopped next to his chair and looked down at him. Murder filled her usually placid green eyes. Suddenly Seth wondered if he'd offended her somehow.

Realizing his feet were still on the desk, Seth dropped them to the floor. When he did, he caught sight of two bare knees gaping through holes in both legs of Emma's panty hose. A tiny bead of blood dribbled down one shin.

Concerned, he cupped his hand over the telephone receiver. "Are you okay?"

She smiled with all the good humor of a hungry gator and slapped the full coffee cup down on his desk. Steaming black liquid sloshed over the rim and puddled in a muddy ring on his blotter. "Fine."

She didn't look fine as she limped away. With full knowledge that he might be risking bodily harm, he opened his mouth to call her back, but his father's insistent pleas interrupted him.

"Seth? Seth, are you there, son?"

Deciding that giving her a few minutes to pull herself together might be wiser than pushing her right now, Seth let Emma go. "Yeah, Pop, I'm here. Where were we?"

Emma stopped at the door, turned, her expression suddenly inscrutable. Her gaze zeroed in on a pile of folders stacked on his credenza, and she hurried across the room to gather them up, pulled open the drawer and started filing.

His father asked a question about Stingray's navigational systems.

"Hold on a second, Dad." Seth cupped his hand over the phone again, suppressing a frown. She always seemed to be hanging over him when he talked about Stingray. Call him paranoid, but...

"Emma, why don't you go out front and sit down for a while. You look like you could use a break." And he could use some privacy to finish this conversation with his father.

Crouched in front of the file drawer, she looked over

her shoulder at him. Surprisingly, mutiny flashed in her eyes in place of her usual polite acquiescence. "These files—"

"Can wait. Maybe you could round up some fresh flowers for the waiting area. The carnations out there are looking a little wilted."

She opened her mouth—to argue again, Seth was sure. He cut her off with a mild tilt of his head.

"Yes, sir." She rose, albeit stiffly, and headed out of the office.

"You can close that door, too."

"Of course."

Was that sarcasm?

Seth felt a twinge of guilt. Emma knew enough about what went on in this office to know something special was happening. Yet he hadn't included her in Project Stingray.

It wasn't that he didn't trust her. He hadn't included any nonessential personnel. The fewer people who knew a secret, the fewer potential points of failure. Seth was simply playing the odds.

Besides, he was too damned distracted when she was around. How was he supposed to concentrate with all of his blood puddled somewhere south of his brain?

Keeping her away from Project Stingray was the smart thing to do. But Emma was no dummy. She knew when she was being summarily dismissed. And when she was being humored with busywork.

She closed the office door a little too hard on her way out.

Seth sighed. "About that nav system, Pop."

Seth talked submarines with Russ Evans for another twenty minutes. By the time he hung up, he'd lost the battle with the headache he'd been trying to stave off.

Damn it, every time they worked out one problem with the Stingray design, three more cropped up. He could solve those—it was just a matter of patience and attention to detail.

But this speed issue was another matter. How in the hell was he going to add enough power to drive the sub four knots faster without increasing the size of the engine?

Seth stood, stretched and paced across the room. This wasn't a problem he was going to be able to solve in his office. He needed to clear his mind, think outside the box.

At his window he looked out across the three blocks of commercial buildings, the thin canal which led to Emerald Cove winding among them, past the beachfront, with its swarm of sun worshippers paying homage to their god, out to the great expanse of water that stretched to the horizon.

Long before he'd been a businessman, he'd been a seaman. Some of his earliest memories were of boating trips with his father. The ocean provided the foundation on which Evans Yachts was built. It was there that he would find his answers. With the salt spray in his face and sea air in his lungs.

Struck by a bout of claustrophobia, Seth dumped his suit coat on the back of his chair, took off his tie, rolled up his sleeves and traded his socks and wingtips for a pair of deck shoes he kept in his office closet.

He paused in his doorway, looking at Emma. His stomach muscles contracted at the sight of her. Damn, how did she do that to him?

"Leaving?" she asked, her voice stony enough to make it clear she knew her place. And that he'd been the one to put her there, solidly, this morning.

His gut twisted around a barb of guilt. "I'm going to take the catamaran out."

She checked her watch. "You have a one o'clock with Hank Petersen."

"I'll sail to Marina del Car. He'll be impressed as hell and I need the air."

"I'm sure he will. And you do." Judging by the way she picked up a nail file and attacked a chipped fingernail the way he would go after a fallen tree with a buzz saw, he'd say she could use a little fresh air, too.

His gut clamped down a notch tighter. What he was thinking was a bad idea. A really bad idea. He was having enough trouble keeping a professional perspective around her here in the office. Out on the waves, with the wind in her hair, the sun glinting off her unfathomable green eyes, he wouldn't be responsible for his own actions.

Besides, she wasn't dressed for sailing.

She quit hacking at her nail and angled her chin toward him. "Anything I can do for you while you're gone? Polish the furniture in the lobby? Wax the floors? Scrape the barnacles off the bottom of the *Pisces?*"

He leaned against the doorjamb. My, my. She was in a mood, wasn't she?

"Actually, Ms. Carpenter, I have slightly less demanding plans for you for the next few hours," he found himself saying without consciously deciding to speak.

He ignored his stomach's warning rumble. He shouldn't be doing this. He had enough on his mind already without adding his secretary's problems. And Emma was in a dangerous mood, albeit one he found intriguing, and that made her more of a distraction than ever.

His sense of self-preservation told him to leave her alone, let her work out whatever was bothering her on her own.

Unfortunately for his sense of self-preservation, right now a distraction sounded like exactly what he needed.

What the hell...

"You wouldn't happen to have a change of clothes with you, would you?" he asked. "Something a little less..."

He smiled, lifted one eyebrow. "Just a little less."

Two

The pirate captain braced against the wheel of the captured frigate. His crisp shirt, open at the collar and stark white against his swarthy complexion, popped in the wind like the sails overhead. With his straight, brilliant smile and noble features, he could have been a gentleman. A man of means with his own sailing ship.

He could have been, but for the lock of sandy brown hair that fell over his forehead to his eyes, branding him forever a rogue—

"Did you hear me, Emma? I said prepare to come about. That means it's time for you to duck!"

Emma leaped two or three centuries ahead in time at the sound of Seth's voice. There she'd gone again, daydreaming.

In an instant he transformed from the handsome pirate captain to the modern-day CEO.

But he was still handsome.

At least her fantastical adventures kept her mind off her stomach, and the endless, nauseating roll of the sea. What had she been thinking, going sailing with her landlubber stomach?

She'd be thinking it might be a good time to make small talk with him. Get him to give up some details for Yankovich. Only now that they were out here, she wasn't much up to conversation.

Winds were southerly, but brisk, and as they tra-

versed southward through the cove to Marina del Car
on the port tack, the chop was vicious. The starboard
tack wasn't much better, as each wave lifted the stern
and pitched them forward like a roller coaster car on
a downhill slope.

With one fist pressed between the hem of her gray
spandex exercise top and the waistband of the matching shorts—the only change of clothes she'd had at
the office—she shouted up at him, "I know how to
sail, you know!"

The mainsail shivered overhead as Seth's forty-foot
luxury catamaran, *Strictly Business,* turned head-to-
wind. Eyes wide, she ducked until her ears were between her knees as the boom breezed by just inches
above her head.

When she looked up, Seth grinned at her. "Good.
Then be a hand and haul in that starboard sheet, would
you?"

The rat.

Back on the port tack, she clenched her teeth against
the incessant pounding of the catamaran's twin hulls
on the surf and climbed into the cockpit with Seth.

His eyes were warmer, more open than they'd ever
appeared in the office as he offered her a steadying
hand, and her stomach lurched for a reason that had
nothing to do with motion sickness. He was different
out here. With his tie off and a sincere smile on, he
was more approachable. Less godlike and more mere
mortal.

More male.

Realizing that her hand was still in his, and that her
fingers were tingling, she pulled away and took a seat
on the aft bench. "Enjoying yourself?" she asked, as

much to take her mind off the sensation that had passed from his hand to hers as anything else.

"Immensely. You?"

She stubbed the toe of her aerobics shoe into the deck. "Maybe we should have taken the *Pisces*."

"My father's floating palace? Nah. Hank Petersen fancies himself a true man of the sea. He wouldn't trust a sailor who motored into port on a million-dollar yacht with GPS and autopilot." Seth winked at her. "Besides, why drive a bus, even a very expensive, luxurious bus, when you can be behind the wheel of an Indy car?"

"For the smoother ride?" she mumbled, a wave of sickness rising in her like the tide.

Seth peered at her a long second. She crossed her arms over her middle, feeling exposed in her clingy tank top and shorts that fit like skin. Awareness flared within her, and she thought she saw it reflected in his amber-brown eyes, as well, before he yanked his gaze away. "You do look a little green around the gills. Don't tell me you get seasick?"

She tipped her chin into the wind and breathed deeply, through her nose. "All right, then. I won't tell you."

His face crinkled. "For God's sake, why didn't you say so before we set out?"

"You didn't give me much of a chance. Besides, I thought we were just cruising down the coast to Mr. Petersen's dock. How was I to know you wanted to go play in the middle of the Atlantic Ocean, and then we'd be facing a head wind and have to tack back and forth for miles to get back?"

She knew she was being unreasonable. It was his boat. His right to go play in the ocean if he wanted to. And she should have told him about her propensity for motion sickness.

She just hadn't been herself this morning.

She gritted her teeth as they bounced over a particularly large swell.

Seth rolled his shoulders, a move she'd seen him make a hundred times when he came to a decision. "All right, all right. The ride is pretty rough. It's that tropical depression down in the Bahamas kicking up the surf. We'll lower the sails and motor back to the marina, how's that? Ought to smooth out the ride some."

Feeling like a heel for spoiling his fun, Emma tried not to sound happy as she turned to climb out of the cockpit. "Head us windward, I'll get the sails."

Two strong hands on her waist lifted her, brought her back against a hard chest and harder slab of abdomen. "You take the wheel," Seth said, putting her hands on the helm. "I'll handle the sails."

A weak breath shivered out of her when he turned her loose. "Sure," she whispered as she watched him pull himself up on deck, admiring the play of male muscle and sinew more than a seasick woman should. "Whatever you say."

Minutes later Seth was back behind the boat's controls, and the engines coughed to life. Emma sunk down into the cockpit bench, stretched her feet out along the seat and tipped her head back, eyes closed.

"How's your stomach?" Seth called as they picked up speed.

"Mmm." She rubbed her palm over her navel. "Bubble, bubble, toil and trouble."

"Well, if you have to vomit, do it in the water," he said, but he didn't sound mad. He sounded sympathetic. And slightly amused. "I'm on a heading straight to the marina. We should be there in twenty or thirty minutes."

The more Emma thought about time, the slower it passed. Instead she thought about standing in a field of daisies. A perfectly still field of daisies. But then an imaginary wind kicked up and the daisies started to sway. Back and forth.

Back and forth.

Emma swallowed and breathed through her nose again.

She thought about a blue sky, dotted by puffy white clouds. But then the clouds began to drift. Back and forth.

She squeezed the guardrail beside her until her fingers went numb.

She thought about one of the several farmhouses she'd bounced between as she'd been growing up. She visualized the rambling, weathered old clapboard frame with narrow stairs up to her attic bedroom. But then she...

Smelled smoke?

Emma opened her eyes and lifted her head. Seth stood in front of her, his back to her, shoulders relaxed, apparently unconcerned.

She crinkled her nose, sniffed again.

There! The faint acrid odor. Coming from the engine compartment on a thin gray cloud.

"Fire!" Her feet thunked onto the deck. "Seth, there's a fire!"

Seasickness forgotten, she was on her feet, reaching for the extinguisher mounted beside the engine room hatch even before he turned. He brought himself alongside her in one long stride, took the red canister from her hands. "Get back!"

She stumbled aft, couldn't stay there and do nothing, and stepped forward again, staying behind him, fisting her hand in the back of his crisp cotton shirt.

Seth pulled the ring on the fire extinguisher and reached for the hatch.

"Be careful," she warned, her fingers tightening on his shirt.

He touched the metal handle to the compartment once, jerked his hand away as if it was hot, then reached back and yanked the door open.

A cloud of black smoke engulfed them. Emma coughed. Her eyes watered; her nostrils stung.

Thankfully, Seth seemed unaffected. He advanced on the engine like a sword fighter on his opponent, the nozzle of the fire extinguisher held before him like a rapier. A second later a white cloud of fire retardant hissed forth, mixed with the black smoke, and then all went quiet.

Seth's shoulders sagged. The extinguisher fell to his side. "It's out."

Emma let go of his shirt and clutched her hand to her chest. "Thank God."

Seth crouched, peering into the clearing compartment. "I don't know what the hell happened. These engines were just serviced."

He waved his hands to sweep away the last of the smoke, then his back went rigid. "What the—" He leaped up, twisting in midair to face her. "Jump!"

"What?"

"Get off the boat! Do it now!" He pushed her to stern.

"Seth, you—"

Before she could tell him he was crazy, he grappled onto her waist and threw her bodily toward the water. She tried to hang on to him, but succeeded only in lessening the force of his throw enough that she wouldn't clear the boat. As she careened toward the water, her ears rang from a loud explosion. A flash of fire spewed from the engine compartment.

Emma watched in disbelief as Seth flew through the air, thrown much higher than her by the blast.

Then her body hit the chilly water, her temple hit the port pontoon and she saw nothing but black.

"Emma!" Seth roared. He choked with the effort, coughed up seawater and called again. "Emma!"

He swirled his arms as he treaded water in the black sea, spinning around to search the surface for sign of her. A dozen yards away, *Strictly Business* listed badly, her port nacelle in flames, the inflatable life raft she carried on that side melted into the hull.

There was still time to climb on board and gather supplies before she went down, though. The flare gun. Life jackets.

God, why hadn't he made Emma wear a life jacket? Why had he brought her at all? To indulge his curiosity about the body that lay under all those frumpy business clothes?

He might have killed her, for God's sake.

"Emma!"

Only the lap of waves, crackle of the fire and gurgle of a sinking boat answered. Bits of fiberglass and marine plywood floated around him. Shards of splintered plastic. A coffee carafe from the galley and a lampshade from the stateroom.

But there was no sign of Emma.

"No. Damn it. No!" He slapped at the water, then dragged in a deep breath and dived.

The water was murky. Below three or four feet, all he saw was blackness. Kicking furiously, he swam along the line between light and dark. The water in his ears echoed his painful heartbeat back to him.

He'd killed her.

She was young and beautiful and she'd had a bad morning and he'd killed her for it. The urge to let go, to sink away into the blackness, tugged at him. He propelled himself to the surface, gulped in another breath and dove again.

He had to find her.

A rope snaked out of the dark depths ahead, one end weighted by something, sinking, the other struggling toward the surface, toward the light.

He grabbed hold of the line, tugged. A plank rose beneath him, the line tangled around it. Then the plank turned over slowly. On the other side, snared in the line like seaweed in a fishing net, Emma's lifeless body hung.

Gripping her beneath her arms, he worked the rope from around her legs and kicked toward the surface. The breath exploded out of him when he reached air. "Emma, talk to me. Say something."

Her face was pale, her skin as translucent as the inside of a clamshell.

Quickly he flipped her to her back, supported her with one hand between her shoulder blades and tipped her head back with the other while he pumped his legs furiously to keep them both afloat.

"Come on, baby. Breathe."

She floated limply in front of him, still as death, no rise or fall to her chest.

His heart jackhammering at twice the speed of his flailing legs, he pinched her nose shut, pulled her close and clamped his mouth down over hers, blowing his breath into her. His downward force drove them both underwater, but Seth didn't care. As long as he was pushing air into her lungs, she wasn't taking in water.

He kicked until they rose to the surface, sucked in another raw breath and descended on her again. Again the water closed over them, silent, ominous, as his lips crushed hers.

Straining with the effort of swimming and breathing for them both, his thighs and his lungs on fire, Seth struggled for daylight. He couldn't keep this up much longer and he knew it. Eventually his strength would run out and he and Emma both would simply drift away.

But not yet.

Cursing the fates, the gods of the sea and fools like himself, he drew in a final breath, melded his lips to Emma's and exhaled that breath from his lungs to hers.

The hand he'd held beneath her shoulders slipped up to cradle the back of her head. His lips moved over hers, coaxing, begging.

Please, baby, breathe.

She jerked beneath him. Her knees drew sharply up, colliding with his midsection. Still holding her nose shut, his lips covering hers so that she wouldn't suck in seawater with her first breath, he kicked with all the energy he could muster.

They broke the surface in a mutual sputter and gag.

"Seth, what— How—"

He tipped her onto her back again, his hands supporting her from underneath. A shudder racked his shoulders as he realized how close he'd come to losing her. "Easy, Emma."

She coughed. "Oh, I don't feel so good." Her lips were blue and her teeth chattered.

He pulled her to a vertical position and wrapped his arms around her. Their legs bumped, tangled. She burrowed closer, sliding a leg between his thighs and finding a kicking rhythm that complemented his.

"You're seasick, remember?" he said, his voice rough. Damn, but she felt good in his arms. Alive. Her hips nestled perfectly against his, ground against him erotically with each ocean swell that buoyed them.

She buried her cheek against the side of his neck. "I don't get sick when I'm *in* the water." An instant of silence passed, then her back stiffened. She lifted her head. "Seth, we're in the water."

He chuckled. He couldn't help it. He was just happy to see the bewilderment in her catlike green eyes. Happy to see anything but death there.

He swept back a lock of hair matted to her forehead. "Yeah, we are."

"The boat…?"

"Exploded."

Her breath hitched. "Exploded?"

He nodded.

She looked around, but there was nothing to see but miles of ocean. *Strictly Business*'s starboard pontoon broke the endless blue a bit, but the remnants of the catamaran wouldn't stay afloat for long, that much was obvious. They were on their own.

Emma lowered her head back to Seth's shoulder. "Oh, I really don't feel so good."

He shook her lightly. "Come on, now. Stay with

me. You took a little knock on the head, but you're going to be fine.''

"Fine?" Her voice rose an octave. "Fine? We're in the middle of the Atlantic Ocean without so much as a rubber ducky. What makes you think I'm going to be fine?"

If her temper was any indication, she was getting her strength back. That was good. She was going to need it.

"We're not in the middle of the Atlantic," he explained patiently. "Just seven or eight miles offshore."

She raised her head, anger gone, real concern set in. "You think either one of us can swim seven or eight miles in this chop?"

He scanned the horizon. He couldn't see Emerald Cove. But behind him he caught a glimpse of the island they'd passed some fifteen minutes ago. Just a blip of green rising out of the sea in the distance.

"We'll make for the island, then. Probably some Coast Guard chopper will pick up our Sarsat beacon and come to pluck us out of the water before we get halfway there, but we'll start. Just in case."

The emergency beacon was designed to begin emitting a distress signal as soon as it submerged. Help was probably already on the way.

Probably.

Emma took another long look at the span of water between her and Seth and the island, and nodded solemnly. "Just in case."

"Think you can swim?"

She smiled bravely. "Think you can keep up?"

Hearty words, but Seth knew better. The shock and trauma of what she'd been through were going to catch up with her. That bump on the head was rising to quite a knot already; she could have a concussion. Her strength wouldn't last long in these rough seas.

But for now it was best to keep her confidence up. He grinned. "Show me what you got, woman."

Three

Emma held out longer than Seth thought she would. They alternated swimming and survival floating for what seemed like days, but probably didn't total more than sixty minutes. Emma's strokes gradually became shorter, her breathing ragged.

Seth had expected that. But he didn't expect her eyelids to sag like those of a child who'd been kept up past her bedtime. The possibility that she might have a concussion burned like a slow-acting poison in his bloodstream. It ate away at his conscience. Flooded his system with guilt.

Finally, when her legs stopped kicking, her arms no longer pulled her through the battering waves and her mouth sank below the waterline, her breath bubbling out, he took her into a rescue hold and towed her. The island loomed close enough for him to make out a strip of sand along the rocky shoreline, a few individual trees inland. They'd made good progress, but they were fighting the current.

Now the fight was his alone.

He swam until his arms ached and his legs dragged him to the bottom like lead sinkers on a fishing line. Until there was nothing but him and the next wave.

And Emma.

"Still with me, Ace?" he asked, battling exhaustion.

"Betcha." She managed a saucy tone, but the slurred words gave away her exhaustion.

He carefully enunciated so she wouldn't hear the same exhaustion in his. "Good girl. We're almost there."

She rolled sideways to get a look ahead, nearly dunking him. "It's so far."

"Optical illusion. Looks farther than it really is."

"Unless it's farther than it really looks."

"Just keep paddling."

He tucked her close to his body and held his breath while the next wave swamped them, then flipped her to her back and pulled her into the rescue hold again.

"We're not going to make it."

Doggedly he stroked toward shore. "Whad'ya wanna bet?"

"Bet? You think this is a game?"

"Nope. Serious. Dead serious, you might say. So what do I get if I win?"

"Like I have anything you want, Mr. Millionaire."

His disbelieving laugh turned into a gurgle, then a sputter when he took a mouthful of water. "Emma, believe me. You have many things I want."

She was silent for a moment. Only a moment. "Like what?"

A swell lifted him until his hips bumped her backside. Why did he have to notice how perfectly she fit into the curve above his hip? His forearm tightened reflexively over her chest. His ego might wish to attribute the hardened peaks of her flattened breasts to his touch, but common sense told him her response was more the effect of the chilly water.

Gritting his teeth, he craned his head around to get

a glimpse of her and adjusted his grip on her to a less, ah, familiar spot.

Her eyes widened in realization.

He set his sights on the island again. "Kick, Emma. Kick."

She did, to little avail. "We're not going to make it."

He bit back his agreement. Their safe haven looked farther away than ever. "We'll make it."

"What makes you so sure?"

"Miami triathlon champion, 'Ninety-six, 'Ninety-eight and 'Ninety-nine."

"Hmph. Macho man."

"You bet, baby."

She didn't sound particularly convinced, but she kicked a little harder.

By the time Seth's feet hit bottom near the island, even he thought it was a miracle they'd made it. With the last of his strength, he dragged Emma to dry sand, then flopped on his back next to her.

"Show-off," she gasped.

"Damn straight," he gasped back.

Eventually their labored breathing eased.

"What do we do now?" Emma asked.

He rolled to his side and propped himself up on his elbow. Frowning, he touched the goose egg on her left temple. That was a hell of a knock she'd taken. But her eyes were clear and she seemed coherent enough.

When she flinched at his probing, he drew his hand back. "We wait for the Coast Guard to find us."

"If they don't? If they aren't even looking?"

He cupped the side of her face, saying another short, silent prayer when he felt the life within her. The warmth. "*Strictly Business* has—*had*—a brand-new

Sarsat-Cospas beacon. The best made. Help is probably already on the way.''

"Unless it malfunctioned.''

"I just had the boat serviced. All the equipment checked out.''

"Including the engines?''

Her bright green eyes darkened to the shade of shadowed forests. He realized he was stroking her neck with his thumb, relishing the pounding of her pulse, and pulled his hand away.

"Including the engines," he confirmed.

The corners of her mouth crooked down. "Maybe you should consider hiring a new mechanic.''

His smile was instantaneous and unstoppable. She'd managed to surprise him again. Not many women could. He liked that about her. After all she'd been through, she deserved the truth.

"The engines didn't malfunction, Emma.''

"Then what...?''

"There was a device in the engine compartment. Plastique of some kind. Pretty sophisticated stuff.''

"A bomb? But who would do that? Who would want to kill us?''

"I don't know.''

But he had a pretty good idea why. Stingray. A lot of America's enemies would like to see the project deep-sixed. A lot more would like to get their hands on the plans.

That thought tugged on a new worry like a marlin on a fishing line. His family...

Even with him out of the way, someone would have to get past his dad, probably his brother Holt, too, to get to Stingray. What if someone had planted similar surprises for them?

Emma frowned. Her concern carved an endearing little vee between her brows. "And if whoever planted the bomb also tampered with the Sarsat beacon...?"

"Then we could be here awhile."

Emma was right. No one would go to the trouble to plant a bomb and leave the emergency locator intact. He rolled away from her and sprawled on his back again before he gave in to the almost irresistible urge to smooth away the creases in her forehead. "A good long while."

His stomach churned sickly. He was well and truly stranded. There was nothing he could do for his family right now. He couldn't protect them. Couldn't take care of them.

But he could damn sure take care of Emma.

"Come on, baby. Burn for me."

Emma crouched next to Seth while he ground the end of a stick against a rock by rubbing it between his palms. "You really think you can start a fire that way?"

"Tom Hanks did it," he said without looking up.

She rubbed her arms, smoothing over the pebbled flesh. Cripes, she was cold. "It took Tom three days."

His face darkened, making her feel bad for doubting him. He rolled the stick faster. "Why don't you go gather some more wood?"

"We don't even have a fire yet."

"It's not for the fire. We need to make the S.O.S. sign on the beach bigger, more visible from the air in case we can't get this blasted signal fire burning. Go."

Emma went, leaving him puffing out tiny breaths into the uncooperative pile of dry grass and twigs. Even marooned on a deserted island, she was doing his fetching, she thought as she plodded away. She supposed she owed it to him, though. He had saved her life.

She wondered if he would have bothered if he'd known the truth about her. Known she'd been sent to spy on him.

Wondering wasn't going to get them rescued, so she concentrated on her search for wood. With any luck, Seth would never know the truth. She would finish her assignment and be gone with him none the wiser for it.

And her career much the better for it.

She just hoped she could live with herself afterward.

This spy thing wasn't turning out to be exactly what she'd thought it would be.

Walking on, she picked up a few branches from the trees beyond the beach, added some palm fronds, then when she bent over a larger fallen limb, she noticed something strange. A bare spot in the grass. A long, narrow bare spot.

She trotted back to the beach. "Seth, come look at this."

"In a minute." He was the picture of concentration. She hadn't seen him so focused since the time, three months ago, when his profit and loss statement wouldn't balance. "I've almost got the fire."

"But it's going to be dark in a minute."

Seth leaned over his rock, blew lightly and waited. Nothing.

Sighing, he straightened. "What is it?"

"I found a path."

"Probably just an animal trail."

Emma frowned. She hadn't thought about wildlife.

Didn't want to. Not when it would be dark in a few minutes, and they had no fire.

"Well, come on. Let's have a look," Seth said, standing and tugging her toward the trees.

She pointed out the path to him and they followed it to a clearing about two hundred yards off the beach. In the soft light of dusk, Emma could barely make out the simple thatch hut that stood in the middle of the open space. "A house!"

"Not exactly a house," Seth said, testing the floor before he stepped past the canvas curtain that served as a door. The walls weren't really walls, but slats that could be propped open with sticks to turn the place into a gazebo. Seth raised one panel and dust motes danced on the sunlight that streamed in as he circled the room slowly, surveying their find.

"Who do you suppose built it?"

"Whoever owns the island, I guess."

Excitement zinged through her. "Do you think they'll come back?"

Seth picked up a can of Campbell's soup from the crates stacked as shelves in one corner and blew a layer of dust off the top. "I wouldn't count on it."

"At least we have a roof. And a floor," Emma mumbled, remembering Seth's animal trail comment.

He strolled outside and she inventoried the contents of the crates, muttering to herself. "Camping supplies. An empty canteen. Mosquito netting."

That might come in handy.

The next shelf held more personal items. Paperback mystery novels. A blank notebook. A Snickers bar that was hard as a rock.

And a Sterno lantern.

Excitement spiked Emma's pulse. Where there was a lantern, there should be…

She shoved a pile of assorted odds and ends aside.

"Matches!" Gleefully she rattled the red-and-blue box, pleased by the full sound. "We've got matches!"

"Well, hallelujah," Seth said, standing in the doorframe. "Looks like today's our lucky day, because we've got fresh water, too. There's a tarp strung in a tree out back as a rain catcher. Spout pours it down into a wooden barrel. It's half-full."

Emma did a pirouette, the weight of the day's misfortunes lifted. "We're saved!"

Hands in his pockets, Seth shuffled into the hut. The waning sunlight threw shadows over his face, giving him an edgy look that matched his tone of voice. "No thanks to me."

"Because you couldn't start a fire from sticks and stones, or make fresh water appear from thin air?" she joked. "What kind of superhero are you, anyway?"

"God, Emma. I almost got you killed. Don't flatter me."

"You saved my life. You pushed me off the boat before it exploded. Untangled me from that rope dragging me down. You *breathed* for me, Seth. I think that deserves a little flattery."

His hands balled into fists in his pockets. "We don't have any food."

She almost felt sorry for him. He was the CEO, used to being in control. But this situation was beyond control. "We can climb for coconuts. Make a trap and catch crabs. And there might be some edible berries and roots in these woods."

His footsteps thudded on the hollow floor as he crossed the room to stand before her. Inches away, he studied her. His dark scrutiny lit up her nerves like spotting flares. "I suppose I could whittle a fishing pole. Find something here to use as a hook."

Feeling his nearness intensely on her hypersensitized skin, in her breasts, she crossed her arms over her chest and smiled gamely. "See, it'll be a big adventure."

"This isn't Robinson Crusoe."

"More like *Gilligan's Island.*"

That got a smile out of him. His white teeth flashed in the looming dark. "Please don't tell me I'm Gilligan."

She stifled a giddy giggle. "More like the professor. All brainy and serious."

"Brainy and serious, huh?"

He took another step forward, a dangerous look in his eyes; instinctively she stepped back.

"Who are you?" he asked, his voice huskier than it had been. "The wholesome farm girl Mary Anne? Or Ginger, the voluptuous tease?"

His broad hands settled on either side of her waist, his fingertips brushing bare skin above the top of her shorts. Her stomach muscles rippled in reaction.

Lord, she was in over her head with this man. She didn't know whether to fall into his arms or run screaming into the night. The air in the room suddenly seemed too thin. She gulped in a breath. "Did I ever tell you I was born on a farm? A pig farm, actually. In Des Moines."

His hands tensed on her waist. "Your *résumé* said you were from Maryland."

Maryland. Right. Her cover story. Cripes, how could she have forgotten? *Because Seth Evans did crazy things to her mind.* "Sure. My family had a farm in Iowa, though. We spent summers there."

"A pig farm."

"Right." She ducked under Seth's arm, grabbed two cups from the camping dishware on the shelves and made a beeline for the water barrel. "Guess that makes me Mary Anne."

She was stranded on a deserted island with a man— a powerful, attractive, magnetic man—who thought she was his secretary. The situation was complicated enough without him thinking of her as...Ginger.

Mary Anne. Wholesome. Sweet. And plain as a double scoop of vanilla ice cream. If Emma was going to get through this and complete her assignment, she had to think like Mary Anne. Act like Mary Anne.

Convince Seth Evans she *was* Mary Anne.

Midmorning the next day, Seth threw another branch on the signal fire and sat on the beach brooding under the pretense of watching for rescue ships.

He didn't like the time he was losing on Project Stingray while he sat out here. He didn't like not knowing whether his family was okay. And he definitely didn't like the way his thoughts kept wandering to his secretary.

She was an employee, for God's sake. It wasn't professional. It wasn't ethical.

But Lord, Emma was a magnificent creature. Not just her body, which had been tantalizing him ever since she'd changed into that skimpy workout getup for their sailing trip. Or her hair, which defied any containment in a ponytail or knot, and massed wildly around her head in a glorious crown of curls. The kind of curls that wouldn't slip through a man's hands when he grabbed on.

It was her courage that attracted him. Her heart.

He tried to think of another woman he knew who could have been thrown from an exploding boat, knocked unconscious and nearly drowned, as Emma had yesterday, and still stood in the hut last night and teased him about *Gilligan's Island*.

He couldn't name one.

That fact spoke volumes about the kind of women Seth had been seeing. And about Emma.

Unfortunately, it did nothing for his peace of mind. He wasn't the only one who felt something between them, some connection. He'd seen the awareness in her eyes when she caught him looking at her. When he caught her looking at him. They were like too rudderless ships headed right for each other. Sooner or later, collision was inevitable.

Scanning the horizon, he prayed for a rescue vessel, a boat, plane, chopper, anything. Willed one to appear.

God help him and Emma both if it didn't appear soon.

Their second full day on the island, Emma thought as she swept the hut floor with a palm frond broom, and still no sign of rescue.

She was hopeful, though. Tomorrow was Monday. People would notice when she and Seth didn't show up at work. They'd see the catamaran missing and call the authorities. A full-scale search would be launched by midafternoon.

That meant she had to work quickly if she hoped to get any information from Seth before their rescuers showed up. She felt like a heel for deceiving the man who had saved her life, for using such dire circumstances to weasel information out of him. But their circumstances weren't really all that dire. They had a roof over their heads, fresh water, plenty of crabmeat and candlelight to eat it by.

The island was actually kind of...homey. Definitely homey.

She refused to think of it as romantic.

Mary Anne would never think of it as romantic.

Soon they would be back in the real world. Seth would don a conservative suit and too-tight tie and she'd go back to a bland skirt and grandmother shoes. She'd never get anything out of him then.

Friday Yankovich would want a report. This surreal timeout on the island provided her a unique opportunity. Seth felt guilty for dragging her along on his misadventure, and he was bored.

He might actually talk to her.

Maybe together they could figure out who had tried to kill him.

She still didn't like the deception, but it was necessary if she was going to complete her mission.

And she *was* going to complete her mission.

Especially now that it included saving Seth's life.

Seth used a few precious cups of rainwater to wash the soot from his face and arms, the stench of smoke from his nostrils, then escaped the blazing midday sun inside the cool shade of the hut.

"The signal fire is going good," he told Emma. "Should burn through the afternoon."

"Great." She combed her hair away from her face with her fingers, and his body hardened like a mainsail running downwind.

He cut his gaze to safer ground. The floor.

"So what do we do while we wait?"

"Same thing we did yesterday—nothing," he grumbled, irritated at his own childishness. He was a grown man, for God's sake. He could make eye contact with a woman without turning into a mutant hormone.

He looked up, met the sea-green depths of her eyes and nearly groaned at the physical ache it caused. Maybe he should have stayed with the fire. Two days of forced proximity—and her dressed in nothing but a skimpy exercise outfit—had driven his crazy attraction for her straight into obsession.

Emma swept across the room on a breeze full of fresh salt air and sunshine. "There must be some better use of our time." She tapped her cheek. "Tomorrow is Monday. What's on your schedule?"

"Huh?"

"Appointments. Meetings. Who are we going to need to reschedule?"

"Really, Emma. This can wait."

Looking insulted, she checked her wrist as if she had on a watch. "You have something else to do right now?"

He plopped onto the floor, drew his knees up and circled them with his arms. He had no idea where she was going with this, but if it was that important to her, he'd play along. Maybe a little work would keep his mind off his family.

And her body.

Emma sat across from him Indian style, holding pencil and paper she must have found in the hut somewhere.

"All right," he said. "We'll have to contact Petersen, of course. See if we can get another date with him.''

She licked the tip of her pencil and made notes on her scrap of yellowed paper. He smiled despite himself. God, she was cute.

''Okay, what else?''

He rattled off two other appointments.

Another note. ''After that?''

''I don't remember.''

She gazed into space as if picturing his calendar. ''Holt asked for thirty minutes.''

Seth rolled his eyes. ''He wants his boat for the regatta. Put him off. It won't be ready for another couple of weeks.''

''What else?''

He caught a scowl before it formed—just barely. He'd been planning on working on Stingray, of course. She couldn't have known that. Yet there was something in the way she asked. Too casual.

''Voice mail, e-mail, correspondence. The usual,'' he answered, mimicking her nonchalance.

''Oh.'' She scratched another note, then set her tablet aside. Unfolding her legs in front of her, she put her hands on the floor behind her, arched her spine and let her head fall back, stretching.

The position exposed the ivory column of her throat, the pulse point just above her collarbone, and thrust her breasts into the air. Her spandex top did little to hide their fullness, the way they rolled with her movements. The upswept peaks at their center.

''I thought you might be planning to spend the morning working with Gideon Faulkner,'' she said.

Seth forgot she wasn't even supposed to know Gideon Faulkner. ''Uh, no.''

"I'm no techno-wizard," she continued as if she hadn't heard him say no. Just how much *did* she know about Gideon? "But I'm a pretty good listener. Maybe you could bounce a few ideas off of me."

Despite the breeze sifting through the open windows, Seth broke a sweat between his shoulder blades. He shook his head at her indifference to his suffering. She had no idea how beautiful she was. No idea what effect she had on him.

"So what do you say?" she asked.

"To what?"

She licked her lips, and Seth sailed beyond familiar territory. He was in uncharted waters now. He'd never been one to let his body rule his mind. It had only taken one bad experience with a woman, years ago, to teach him the dangers of going off half-cocked. He decided when and where to pursue a woman, not his anatomy.

At least he had until he got stranded on a deserted island with Emma Carpenter. It annoyed the hell out of him that she could disable his cognitive functions with nothing but a look.

Done stretching, she sat up. "Fill me in on whatever you and the genius are cooking up. Maybe I can help."

"That's not such a good idea." He was having a hard enough time maintaining a professional distance from her. He didn't want to share his deepest secrets with her.

"If you say so," she said. "But I don't see what it would hurt. We could both use the distraction."

Distraction. Yes. Distraction was a good idea. Work was a good idea. Work would keep him from pulling her into his arms and showing her just how much of a distraction he could provide her.

"You're right. I should be working," he said, scrubbing his two-and-a-half-day stubble with his hands. Emma's eyes filled with hopeful light, then dimmed when he finished his thought. "There's no reason for you to suffer, though. I just have some brainstorming to do."

"I don't mind."

"It's Sunday, Emma." His voice sounded gruffer than he meant it to be. "Your day off. We might be stranded here, but it's still paradise. Why don't you go out and enjoy the beach awhile?"

She dropped her pencil and paper. "Sure. And maybe I could rustle up some fresh flowers for the hut while I'm at it."

She was gone before Seth figured out the reference to the morning they'd set out on their fateful cruise, when he'd excused her—booted her out, more like—from his office while he talked to his father. He supposed he could have been more tactful, then and now. But dammit, he hadn't offended her on purpose. She just...set him on edge in a way no woman had in a long time.

He could go after her, explain himself, but that was a dangerous road. He should be happy she was mad. Mad was safe.

As was distance. He definitely needed distance.

He would sleep on the beach tonight. Claim he needed to tend the fire, even though there wouldn't likely be anyone out to see it. The sand would be lumpy and cold, but hell, it wasn't as if he was going to get a lot of sleep in the hut, either, with her lush body there, just an arm's reach away in the darkness.

Resigned, he picked up the pencil and paper she'd left behind and tried to turn his energy to Stingray. But two hours later, when he looked down at the figures he'd drawn, they didn't look much like a submarine.

They looked very much like an auburn-haired beauty with smoldering green eyes and a body that could set a man on fire.

Damn. He had it bad.

Emma checked the signal fire, then appeased her restless energy by walking down the beach to a rocky point that jutted into the roughening sea like a skyscraper puncturing a thunderhead. With each wave that pounded the rocks, the ocean spray washed over her.

It really wasn't his fault, she decided after a couple of hours of contemplation. She rose gingerly on legs cramped from sitting on the hard stone too long. He had no reason to trust her. In fact, she didn't deserve his trust, though he had no way of knowing that either. Come to think of it, there wasn't much he *did* know about her.

Including how important it was that she get close to Project Stingray. Or that he was the obstacle that stood between her and all her dreams. She'd acted childishly at the hut. Now she wasn't sure what to say to Seth when she got back.

Wondering if she was really cut out for the spy business, she headed back. As she climbed off the rocks, a powerful wave crashed into shore, drenching her in chilled, salty water. The surf hadn't been nearly that violent earlier.

An ominous sense of dread settling in the pit of her stomach, she turned her eyes to the sky. What she saw sent her scurrying to the hut, her reticence to face Seth vanished like a stone tossed into murky water. The first fat raindrops splashed in her face, clung on her eyelashes, even before she reached the door.

She pushed the canvas curtain aside and rushed in. Bent over the writing tablet on the floor, Seth raised his head. For a sliver of a second, something wild and hungry looked at her out of his brown eyes. Then he caught himself, and must have seen her misgiving.

Scowling, he stood. "What?"

"Did you say there was a tropical depression in the Bahamas when we left Emerald Cove?"

"Yeah. But it was supposed to turn north, into open sea."

"I don't think it turned." She calmed herself with a breath. Unbidden, her gaze turned toward the towers of cumulonimbus clouds visible through the wall slats.

"I think it's here."

Four

"It's only a storm, Emma."

Rain lashed the hut's thatch roof. Wind howled through the trees in an alto voice.

Lying on one of the palm frond and fern-leaf pallets they had made the first night, Seth went back to his doodling and worrying about his family, determined to ignore the tempest outside.

And the tempest inside him.

When it came to fury and power, he'd match his libido against Mother Nature anytime. At least any-time he was confined in a twelve-by-twenty hut with Emma Carpenter. Especially Emma Carpenter wearing nothing except two scraps of spandex.

He glanced at her without raising his head. The high humidity curled her wavy hair into a mass of untamed ringlets. Her dripping exercise outfit clung to her curves like a coat of wet paint. A *thin* coat of wet paint.

He caught himself licking his lips and lowered his gaze.

He heard her bare feet pad across the room. She stopped in front of his place on the floor, giving him a really excellent view of her ankles and ten wrinkled, adorable, very sexy toes sporting a hint of pale pink polish on their nails.

Funny, this storm seemed to have arrived on a warm front. His temperature was definitely rising.

"I don't know how you can be so blasé," she chided.

Blasé? If only she knew how nonblasé she made him.

Then again, maybe it was better she didn't know. Otherwise, she'd probably run screaming out of the hut, storm or no storm.

"Little tropical depression's nothing to worry about."

He risked another look up as she moved away from him, her step jerky, anxious. Hooking her finger between the ties that held the canvas door in place, she inched back the heavy sheet to peer outside. A blast of heavy, moist air rushed through the opening, making the flame on the lantern flicker. Outside, lightning cut a jagged tear in the blanket of darkness. The brief flash showed saplings cracking like whips in the wind and larger growth leaning sideways in the onslaught.

He stood and went to her by the door for a better look, but dark had fallen two hours ago, making nature's attack that much more forbidding. Now they couldn't even see the face of their assailant, other than in the surreal strobe of lightning strikes. They could only feel her pounding.

The storm's static electricity charged the air, arced between them as they exchanged a glance. He wondered if Emma could feel it—the barometric pressure dropping around them.

And not because of the storm.

Her face paling, Emma fastened the fabric door and turned away from the gale. "It could be a hurricane by now, for all we know. We've been out of touch nearly three days.''

The storm was definitely worse than he'd thought. Not that he'd admit that to her. She already looked nervous enough to unzip her skin and climb right out. It bothered him to see her so upset. Made him want to comfort her.

Dangerous thought.

''Spoken like a true Iowan,'' he said, carefully masking his own concern in an attempt to belay hers before he did something stupid.

''What's that supposed to mean?''

''I've lived in Florida all my life. Seen plenty of hurricanes. This is just a little squall. The worst that's going to happen tonight is the roof springs a leak and we get a little damp. Why don't you sit?''

''I'll stand, thanks.'' When another blast of wind hit, she turned her back on him, wrapped her arms around herself and shivered along with the walls of the hut.

Seth frowned. He wished he had dry clothes for her.

More clothes for her.

Better yet, a blanket to wrap around her. Cuddle her in.

Her back to him, she jolted when he wrapped his shirt around her. He couldn't help himself. He steadied her with hands on both her shoulders.

''Emma,'' he said close to her ear. ''There's nothing to be afraid of. I promise.''

She turned her fathomless eyes toward him, and his gut tied itself in a bowline. He realized his hands were still on her shoulders. He should let her go, back away.

He didn't. Couldn't.

''I'm not afraid,'' she whispered. But when a gust

of wind lifted a section of thatch roof, then threw it
back in place, and the canvas door popped on the ends
of its ties, her body betrayed her. Her muscles bunched
with every crackle.

"Liar," he said, kneading her quivering flesh.

"I'm not afraid of the storm," she amended. She
tried to turn her head away, but he lifted her chin in
his hand.

"Then what?" he asked.

She didn't have to answer. He saw the truth in her
eyes. Felt it in the tension beneath his touch.

"Beautiful lady," he said, his head lowering to her
until their mouths brushed. Feeling as if he were falling into a deep, deep well, he briefly captured her
lower lip between both his, then released it, but kept
up his nuzzling. "Don't you know I would never hurt
you."

Emma turned into his chest, her hands fisted in his
T-shirt, but she didn't push him away. Her lips moved
in synch with his, sending frantic messages down his
spine. She clutched at his shoulders, his back, as if she
was as lost in the whirlpool of sensation swirling
around them as he was.

It couldn't mean—

Surely she didn't want—

One of her legs lifted to ride the outside of his.

Oh, yeah. She wanted.

He lifted his head, looked deeply into her emerald
eyes. His heart thrummed as loudly as the rain. His
hands speared through the hair behind her head. The
pounding rain washed away the last of his resolve.

"Let me make love to you, Emma. I'll make us both
forget about the storm."

* * *

"I want you, Emma."

God, this couldn't be happening. She couldn't be losing her senses beneath the crescendo of drumming rain, the roar of an angry sea, the rush of wind. But her body had been taken over by a driving need as powerful as the storm. It swept her away, pulled her under.

"Say you want me, too," Seth murmured against her neck. His hands left her hair to glide down her body and up again. When his thumbs brushed the outer slopes of her breasts, his touch warm through the thin material that covered them, a gale of sensation even stronger than the wind shook her to the bone.

All the reasons she shouldn't make love to Seth Evans flashed through her mind like lightning. Vivid. Startling. Elemental.

She'd lied to him about her identity, her purpose. She'd been sent to spy on him. He was her target, her mark.

He wasn't the type to take betrayal lightly. When he found out—*if* he found out—he would be a force to reckon with.

But, like lightning, the reasons she should put a stop to what was happening between her and Seth were gone in the blink of an eye, leaving behind only the faint, burning scent of ozone and hypersensitive nerves.

Seth's callused fingers swept the nape of her neck, lifted her corkscrew curls and tangled in them. He used the hold to tip her head back, exposing her throat to his agile lips and drawing up a moan from deep inside her.

She was a farm girl from Iowa. She'd lived all her

life longing to feel the kind of raw intensity engulfing her now. She wouldn't cower below deck when she could ride the bow, experience all that life had to offer.

He opened his legs and she stepped into the cradle of his thighs.

"I want you, too."

She expected a little more coaxing. Some teasing. A trickle of desire carefully nursed to a stream.

Instead she got a flash flood. Seth's hands shook as they moved, stripping off his shirt and her top with startling fervor. His lips, his teeth clashed with hers. Tugging, tearing, their hands tangled in a rage of passion.

The perfect storm.

Dimly, Emma was aware of the rumble of thunder outside the hut, the vibration of the floor beneath her feet. The splash of a raindrop on the back of her neck. The roof was leaking.

She didn't care.

Seth held the ivory globe of her left breast in his palm, staring at it as if transfixed. He cupped the other, enthralled with both.

"I've wanted to touch you like this since the day I met you."

She looked up at him, suddenly self-conscious. She'd never thought of her body as worthy of a man's lust. But the reverent look in his eyes, the concentration on his face as he rolled one nipple between his thumb and forefinger, gave her confidence.

She arched, pushing herself deeper into his hands. "Then touch me."

Bending her back over his arm, he did. With his lips. With his tongue. With his teeth.

"You taste so good. I want to drink you down," he murmured. "All of you."

He bent to suckle her and she watched over his shoulder as a raindrop splattered between his shoulder blades and ran down the valley of his spine.

"Let me taste you now," she said. Then she nipped at his neck, sipped on his collarbone and dragged her tongue down his sternum. The things she imagined doing to her serious-minded boss shocked her. Inflamed her.

He sunk to his knees, pulling her down with him. Pausing only to snuff out the lamp, he lay her down on the bed of palm fronds. He came on top of her, and she found his back slick with sweat and rainwater when she wrapped her arms around him.

Despite the need coursing through her, she trembled. She was no virgin, but with Seth it was like the first time. Overwhelming.

He held himself above her. "Scared again?"

"No."

"Then what was that hitch in your breath?"

She smiled in the dark. Overwhelmed or not, she wanted this. Wanted him. "Impatience?"

He jolted as if she'd hit him with a twelve-volt charge. Parting her thighs with his knee, he nestled against her. She unbuttoned his slacks, pushed them and his briefs over his hips. He kicked off the cumbersome clothing, then peeled her shorts down her legs an inch at a time, caressing and kissing his way along the path of newfound skin.

Rain pierced the ceiling in a steady drip now. The cool water puddled between Seth's shoulder blades, warming almost before she could wipe it away. If he got much hotter, it might boil.

Crouched between her legs, Seth trailed his hand up the insides of her thighs. She drew her knees up bucking instinctively when his fingers found her pushed her toward oblivion.

Humbled and hungry, she writhed on his hand Moaned on his breath when he leaned down and took her mouth again.

"Come for me, Emma," he murmured against her cheek. "I want to watch."

She shook her head, eyes squeezed shut and hands thrown above her head. Unable to see him in the dark unable to hear him above the vicious battering of the storm, she could only feel him. On top of her. Around her.

Now she wanted to feel him inside her.

"Not without you."

His body tensed on top of her. He raised himself up on his elbows, drew back from her. A ragged breath stuttered out of him. "I can't do this. I'm sorry."

"S-sorry?" She strained to see him, letting out a frustrated gurgle when her eyes couldn't cut through the darkness. A fingernail of panic scraped along her spine. He didn't want her after all?

As if reading her mind, he cupped her cheek gently in his palm. "It's not that I don't want you. I've wanted you since the first time I laid eyes on you."

"Then what?"

"I don't have any protection."

The breath she'd been holding whooshed out of her He wanted her after all. Wanted her so badly she could feel him trembling with the strain of holding himself back.

Damn him, he was always holding back on her.

"Why didn't you ever tell me...how you felt?"

"You work for me, Emma. Office relationships are not a good idea."

"And now?"

"Now we're a long way from the office."

"But you're still holding back." She slapped a fist into his muscled shoulder, horrified at the tears filling her eyes. "You're always holding back on me."

Still poised above her, his body tight as a bowstring, he said, "We're not just talking about sex here, are we?"

Anger howled inside her like a cyclone, growing in intensity. No, they weren't just talking about sex. They were talking about trust. She'd bared herself to him, body and soul. Put herself in the most vulnerable position a woman could put herself in with him, and what part of himself had he given in return?

His protection.

Bah. She didn't want his protection. She wanted him. She wanted to see the same naked need in his eyes she knew he must see in hers.

In one smooth move she flipped him to his back, rolled him off the palm frond bed onto the damp, plank floor.

She straddled him and stroked his erection with the inside of one thigh, bringing him close, oh so close to her portal.

Lightning flashed a warning in his hard, dark eyes. Splaying her hands across his wide chest, she locked gazes with him and sank down on his rigid flesh. "Who says I need protection, anyway?"

Seth's control tightened, pulled unbearably at its tethers, then snapped. He pumped his hips up roughly, impaling her with himself, then turned her over, hooked his arms under her knees and ground himself down on her. Into her.

He gasped at the depth of his penetration. The perfect fit.

"Stingray," he growled, fighting to get the words out over the need to drive himself into her again and again. He knew she wanted more from him. Pretty words about his feelings for her. Love words.

He couldn't give her those. Seth never let his emotions get involved in his affairs and wouldn't compromise himself—or her—by pretending that he did. But he could give her the truth. He could give her what he'd been holding back.

"Wh-what?"

"It's a submarine. The project I've been working on with Gideon Faulkner. I'm sorry I didn't tell you before."

She threw her head back and laughed. "Apology accepted. Now dive, Captain. Dive!"

Not needing a second invitation, he plunged more deeply into her. She rolled, taking him with her, and drove herself down on him. He toppled them again and pushed himself high into her. Their rain-slicked bodies slipped and slid together, the friction electrifying.

She arched, his name on her lips, as the ripples started deep inside her and shuddered outward. Thrusting once more, twice, Seth linked his fingers with hers and tumbled into oblivion with her.

By the time Seth regained the feeling in his extremities, the significance of what he and Emma had done battered his consciousness like the wind against the frail walls of their hut.

He'd had sex with plenty of women over the years. Glamorous women. Exotic women. Rich women. Women who wanted all the comforts his success and lifestyle had to offer and women who just wanted one good night.

Never had he experienced anything like this. Never had he had trouble walking away from a woman's bed when he was through.

Only Emma made him want to stay and do it again. And again. With protection or without, no matter how stupid he knew that to be.

Only Emma made him think that he might still be capable of love for a woman, after all.

Body tensing, Seth savaged that thought.

No. He'd given up on love. Permanently.

Gradually his body chilled in the cooling night air. Sensing the same in Emma, he reached for his shirt and spread it over her shoulders. She curled against his side, one leg thrown over both of his.

"Better?" he asked.

"Mmm."

One soft breast pillowed against his arm, and he reached for it. Such perfection, he thought as he tweaked the tip. Such absolute, exquisite perfection.

Her eyes opened slumberously, and as their breaths grew ragged, she climbed on top of him, took him inside.

Seth may have given up on love. But he'd definitely reaffirmed his healthy respect for lust.

Emma woke to the feel of sunlight warming her closed eyelids and the sound of water dripping steadily into more water.

Understanding came back slowly, along with the

memories of last night. Twisted bodies. Hot breaths.
Murmurs in the dark.

And a leaking roof.

She remembered it all now. She and Seth had
woken to a downpour inside the cabin. They'd set out
plates and buckets to collect the water, then slaked
their thirst for each other before reluctantly putting
their clothes back on to ward off the damp chill.

Smiling, she reached for him, her mind sleepily
spinning a daydream of the captured princess carried
away to the pirate's lair, but her groping hand found
the place next to her on the verdant pallet empty and
cool.

She opened her eyes. Sunlight shone in through the
open slats. A light breeze carried in the scents of seawater, sodden earth and wet vegetation.

Emma turned to her side and drew her knees up,
disappointed that Seth wasn't there to curl up with,
but content for now to review the night in lazy re-
membrance and to inventory each of her body's deli-
cious morning-after aches and tingles.

His shirt hung over her shoulders. She pulled it up
to her nose and inhaled the musky male scent of him
already so familiar to her. She'd had reservations
about sleeping with him, but looking back, she
couldn't regret anything they'd done.

The question was, would he?

Here on the island they could be equals. Lovers. But
in the real world, she was his secretary.

At least, he thought she was.

In the office he set a high standard of professionalism for himself and those who worked for him.
Where would that leave them when they got home?

Never one to leave a question unanswered, Emma stood. She slipped her arms into the sleeves of Seth's shirt, rolled the cuffs up to her elbows and went in search of her missing man.

At the door, she found a note pinned to the canvas. "Gone Fishin.'"

Unaccountably pleased by the sight of the firm strokes of his handwriting, and the fact that he'd cared enough to let her know where he'd gone, she set the note on the shelf and weighted it with the corner of a paperback to keep it from blowing away.

She was about to leave when she saw the larger tablet. The paper Seth had been working on when she'd left the hut yesterday afternoon, and doodling on when she returned.

The submarine?

Biting her lower lip, she debated looking. Seth had shown her the first modicum of trust last night. He'd told her about Stingray and promised to fill her in. He didn't deserve to have her sneaking a look at his notes behind his back.

On the other hand, she had a job to do. Important people expected her to gather information. All the information she could get.

Her hand wavered, then fell to her side.

She couldn't do it.

She backed away before she changed her mind and was just stepping out of the hut when she heard it. A low whine. As it grew louder, it also became sharper.

The mechanical hum of an engine. The whir of props.

An airplane!

Five

Emma ran for the beach in a sprinter's stride. Debris scattered by the storm cut into the soles of her bare feet. Ferns and low-lying limbs snatched at her arms, trying to hold her back. None of it slowed her.

When she broke into the clear she saw the aircraft, a seaplane, hardly more than a speck on the horizon, its tail to her, flying away from the island.

"Come back!" She jumped in the sand and waved her arms. "Please, come back!"

Seth streaked across the edge of the surf toward her, gesturing wildly with his fishing pole. "The fire, Emma! Put more wood on the fire!"

Last night's rain must have doused their signal, she thought glumly as the plane grew smaller in the distance. Seth had restarted it, but the flames weren't up to full strength. The pilot would never see it at this distance, especially behind him, but she gamely threw logs onto the burning pile anyway.

Seth pounded up beside her, his bare chest heaving. "That's enough."

"It's not catching. The wood is wet."

"Wet is good," he huffed. "It'll smoke."

True to his word, the damp logs sizzled when the flames hit them. A column of black smoke twisted into the sky.

"Will he see it?" She tugged the tails of Seth's shirt over her thighs.

He shook his head. "I don't know."

Emma's nerves hummed like high-voltage cables. "Please. *Please.*"

Very slowly, the seaplane angled around. It banked, turned until it faced them directly. Waggling its wings, the seaplane made a beeline for the shore and roared by overhead so low she could almost have reached out and touched the snapping green gator logo on the side.

Emma jumped up and down. "He sees us!"

She wrapped her arms around Seth's neck and leaped, hooking her legs over his hips. He swung her around three times, his broad smile flashing in the sun, then stopped and squinted over her shoulder. "It's Drew."

"I don't care if it's Santa Claus. We're saved. Who's Drew?"

"My cousin."

"Oh," she laughed, giddy with the knowledge that their ordeal was over. She'd never met Seth's cousin, but she'd spoken with him on the phone and knew he ran an air charter service.

Seth squeezed her. "In a little while we'll be back in civilization."

"Chocolate milkshakes."

"Air conditioning."

"A bubble bath."

"My computer."

"Indoor plumbing."

He grinned. "Okay. You win."

As the seaplane touched down on the water and taxied to shore, its props whipped up sand and seawater. Seth pulled Emma's head into the crook of his neck and bent away from the barrage of tiny projectiles, but grit still stung Emma's eyes and stuck between her teeth.

She didn't care.

They were saved.

When the plane's propellers whined to a stop and the air cleared, Seth straightened and Emma opened her eyes.

A man climbed out of the pilot's seat, stepped into the ankle-deep water and threw his headset back inside. He raked a hand through his black hair, standing it on end, and turned toward them. A slow, devilish smile spread across his face as he took them in.

Self-consciously, Emma realized she was still in Seth's arms, her legs around his waist, and struggled to get down.

The pilot—Drew—cocked a hip against one of the plane's struts, crossed his arms over his chest and grinned. "Table for two? I think I have something by the window. Ocean view. Nice and airy."

Seth's spine stiffened. He set Emma gently on her feet, never taking his eyes off his cousin. "What the hell took you so long?"

Drew waded ashore. "Hey, next time you decide to get lost at sea you might want to call ahead and let someone know. We had no idea you were missing until your mother tried to get hold of you yesterday. Even then we weren't sure if there was really a problem or if you were just playing hooky."

"I never play hooky."

"Yeah, that's what your mom said. Couldn't get out to look for you until this morning with that front last night, though. Where the heck is your boat?"

Seth rubbed his hand over his whiskers. "Let's just say the fishes have a nice new condominium."

"You sank a quarter million dollar boat?"

"Not exactly," Seth grumbled.

Drew's brows lifted. Their eyes met and a moment of silent communication passed between the two men.

"Ooo-kay," Drew said.

Emma had watched the byplay between the two men, fascinated, but now she couldn't contain herself any longer. She cleared her throat, waiting for an introduction.

Clearly embarrassed, Seth shuffled a foot to his left, widening the gap between them.

"Hello, pretty lady," Drew said, taking her hand. "I don't believe we've met."

Seth pulled Drew's hand from hers without looking at either one of them. "Emma Carpenter, my overly friendly cousin Drew Evans. Drew, Emma Carpenter."

Surprise—and no small amount of amusement—flashed across Drew's lean features. "Your secretary?"

"My executive assistant," he corrected, and stomped away. "Come on and help me put this fire out so we can get the hell out of here. Emma, if there's anything you want from the hut, now would be a good time to get it."

Emma dug her toes into the beach like a sand crab and watched Seth walk away without a backward glance.

So she was back to fetching for him, huh?

She guessed that answered her question about what would happen once they got home.

* * *

Seth slouched in his office chair and gazed out the window at the sea, refreshed by a forty-minute shower and a shave. If he'd had a decent night's sleep, he might feel human again.

But after three nights on a hard plank floor, his bed had felt much too soft last night. And after one night with Emma curled up beside him, his arms had felt much too empty. He couldn't remember the last time he'd spent an entire night with a woman. The last time he'd wanted to.

On the island, he'd definitely wanted to. He'd wanted to spend the night and the morning and the next afternoon....

He'd wanted to so badly that he'd forced himself to rise with the sun and get out of the cabin before he gave in to the craving to roll on top of her and rouse her with a very special wake-up call.

He'd needed to prove to himself that he could walk away, and he'd done it. Then.

But what about tomorrow? And the day after that?

How was he going to face her every day in the office and not think about what they'd shared? Not want it again?

Seth knew better than to let his heart—or any other part of his anatomy—overrule his head. The Tiffany disaster had taught him the folly of giving himself wholly over to a woman. Taught him well.

They could have his body—it was all most of them wanted, anyway. That and his money. But he knew better than to open up his heart for their inspection and exploitation.

Yet he couldn't shut himself off from Emma. It was like a door had been opened between them and it wouldn't close. He gave her everything. He had pumped himself into her slick heat with a freedom he hadn't felt in years.

He'd told her about Stingray, for heaven's sake.

"Are you sure it was a bomb, son?"

Seth turned from the window to see Russ Evans prop his forearms on the far side of Seth's desk, leaning forward in concern.

"I'm sure, Pop." His problem with Emma would have to wait, Seth thought with a mental sigh. He had business to take care of.

When he returned yesterday, he had wasted no time in letting his father, Holt, cousins Drew and Marcus, and Gideon Faulkner know what had happened aboard the *Strictly Business*. They'd convened a powwow in his office at eight this morning to decide what to do about it. Holt, Gideon and Russ joined him in person. Marcus, a Navy SEAL currently serving in a diplomatic position as well as a proud new dad, dialed in via speakerphone on a secure line from his office in Maryland. He and his wife, Samantha, had returned to the States just two months ago for the birth of their first child.

"Jesus, Seth," Holt said, a scowl darkening his beach-boy good looks. "You could have been killed."

"Emma nearly was." That knowledge sat like a cannonball in his gut.

"What were you doing out there with her, anyway?"

Seth's fingers tightened around his gold Mont Blanc pen. "We were on our way to a meeting."

"Seven miles offshore in a forty-foot catamaran? Wouldn't it have been easier to drive your BMW Z3 down the coast highway?"

Seth shot his brother a quelling look. "Can we get on with this?"

"Yeah. Seems like we ought to focus on who might want to kill you." Marcus's voice crackled over the phone, eliciting grins from the Evans men in the room. Marcus had a way of stating the obvious.

"Double-crossed anybody lately?" Gideon asked Seth, surprising everyone. Gideon didn't usually speak up unless he was asked. Sometimes he seemed almost painfully uncomfortable with people.

Seth guessed spending nearly a whole life a virtual captive could do that to a person.

Avoiding all gazes, Gideon leaned over Seth's desk, playing with one of those perpetual motion executive desk toys.

"If it's not that," he said without looking up, "and you're not in over your head with a loan shark and don't have a greedy wife after your life insurance policy, then I figure maybe the bombing has something to do with Stingray."

Holt stopped his pacing. "Gideon, you sound just like Marcus!"

He looked a lot like Marcus, too. They were like different sides of the same coin, alike in some ways, opposite in others. They shared the same broad shoulders, thick black hair and bright blue eyes. But Marcus carried a lot more muscle than his brother.

Gideon's strength was in his brain.

Even if he had developed a sudden penchant for stating the obvious, just like Marcus.

Gideon hunched his shoulders and went back to staring at the desk toy, but not before Seth caught his grin.

Pleased that Faulkner was finally getting comfortable enough with the group to give them a glimpse of his sense of humor, the corners of Seth's mouth tugged upward a moment, then he tapped his pen on the desk blotter. "Any idea who might be interested in your slick new sub, Marcus?"

"Well." The Evanses waited through the silence. They knew better than to interrupt Marcus while he gathered his thoughts. "My guess would be everybody's favorite international fruitcake, Bruno DeBruzkya. As long as he's cozying up to the folks in the Sharfa peninsula, he's got access to a seaport. Figure that means he's going to want himself a navy."

Holt showed his disgust for the rogue general with a shake of his head. "Sharfa? I thought that province belonged to Holzberg."

"So does the Holzberg government. But the territory's been disputed for generations. Kind of like the Gaza Strip in Israel. There are supporters of both countries living there. Whoever pumps the most money into the area in the form of food and medical supplies tends to have control. Right now that's DeBruzkya. 'Course the two or three thousand Rebelian troops he has stationed in the peninsula don't hurt his control factor, either."

Seth's chair creaked when he leaned back, considering. "What I can't figure is how he thinks killing me is going to help him get a navy."

He sat up again when Holt and his father shared a shifty look.

"What?" Seth asked, eyes narrow.

"We had a little trouble here while you were gone, son."

"There was a robbery attempt," Holt added, then

shrugged. "At least we thought it was a robbery attempt."

Seth blew out a breath. He didn't like anything about this. "We don't keep any cash here. Nothing valuable except a few computers. There are a lot easier targets than Evans Yachts for those kind of goods."

"They weren't after cash or computers," Marcus said, stating the obvious again. "They were after Stingray."

"The bomb was a diversion," his father added.

Holt paced the width of Seth's office, raking his sandy blond hair back from his forehead. "I don't know about this navy project, bro. Maybe it wasn't such a good idea."

"It's going to open up a whole new line of business for us, Holt."

"At what cost? Your life? Your secretary's?" He gestured toward the side pane window next to the closed office door.

Seth looked out, surprised to see Emma striding across the outer office and tossing her purse on her desk. His throat constricted at the sight of her.

She was back to her regular business dress, but somehow it didn't look so prudish and proper now that he was intimately familiar with what lay beneath.

"We can't just pull out of Project Stingray," Seth said, his eyes never leaving Emma. What the hell was he going to do about her? About his unnerving attraction to her? "We've got too much invested."

"It's dangerous."

Seth tore his gaze away from Emma and challenged his brother. "And racing yachts isn't? I don't see you trading in your competition boat for a dinghy."

"That's different."

"Settle down, boys," Russ Evans interrupted.

Seth let out a sigh. "Look. We just need to be more careful, that's all. Marcus, find out what you can about DeBruzkya and his plans. Pop and I will work on bumping up security around here."

"What about me?" Holt asked.

"You've got a race to get ready for."

"You're not leaving me out of this." The baby of the family, Seth thought. Always worried about being left out.

"All right. You keep an eye on things at home."

"I'll set up some navy security there. Unobtrusively, of course. And at Gideon's place, too."

None of them had forgotten DeBruzkya's rumored role in the Coalition that had held Gideon captive and forced him to steal 350 billion dollars from the World Bank for them. American law and the Extraordinary Six had put most of the Coalition behind bars for the foreseeable future, but they hadn't been able to touch DeBruzkya.

Gideon's Adam's apple bobbed. He looked paler than he had a minute ago. "That won't be necessary. I can take care of myself."

"Gid, you gotta let me put some men on the house," Marcus said.

"I said I can take care myself." Gideon's blue eyes flashed with more life than Seth had seen in him before. "I won't be held prisoner in my own house again."

Silence hung in the room like a ticking bomb. Finally Seth's father rose, stepped over to Gideon and put his hand on the man's shoulder. "You've more than proven you can take care of yourself, Gideon. But you have a wife to consider now, too. A baby on the way. Think about them.''

Gideon's whole being softened. His gaze fell to his feet.

"It won't be like before, Gideon," Marcus said softly over the phone. "I swear it."

Holt's gaze shifted uncomfortably between the ceiling, Seth and his dad, then he cleared his throat and did what any good man would do in this situation. He changed the topic. "So what do we tell Mom and Laura?"

"We keep this between us for now," Seth said.

"They have a right to know—"

"The more they know, the more danger they could be in."

"Gotta agree on that one," Marcus threw in.

"Seth and Marcus are right, son. Let your mother and sister be. No need to worry them over this."

Holt's eyes filled with mutiny, but he held his tongue. He might not like it, Seth knew, but Holt would go along with the decision. For now.

"We're settled, then," Seth said, standing. "Let's get to work."

With his father and Marcus taking extra precautions, and Holt watching over the family at home, that left only one person unprotected.

Emma.

Until Stingray was finished, anyone close to him would be at risk.

He knew what he had to do now. Supposed he'd known it all along.

That was why he'd hardly been able to make eye contact with her during their short flight back to civilization. Why he'd packed her off for home in a limo without so much as a by-your-leave after they'd landed.

Faced with the reality of his relationship with Emma, of sharing it with the world, he'd lost his nerve. She worked for him, for God's sake. Employee-employer relationships tended to be very messy affairs, no pun intended.

Best case, they turned warm, friendly working environments into arctic chill zones. Worst case, they became ugly sexual harassment suits to be settled in court.

He couldn't get involved with her. He needed to focus on Stingray now, and on protecting his family.

It would be better, safer, for him and Emma both if they kept their relationship strictly professional.

Now all he had to do was convince her of that.

Emma opted for herbal tea instead of coffee this morning. The last thing her nerves needed was another jolt.

She'd spent most of yesterday hanging up on reporters who wanted the scoop on what it was like to be marooned in paradise with the most eligible bachelor in Florida. She would have disconnected the darn phone if she hadn't been waiting for one special call.

Seth's call.

Their rescue yesterday had come unexpectedly. The hours following had been hectic. She understood how he might not have had time to contact her. But surely when things quieted down, she'd thought, when night fell and he was alone in his condo with nothing but silence to keep him company, when he'd had time to sort through his feelings, he would call.

She'd been wrong.

Then this morning in the lobby, she'd had to fight her way through the hordes of press still hungry for their story. Gus, the security guard, had held them back as best he could. But she'd been jostled and bumped, generally rattled before the elevator doors slid blessedly closed and she was lifted to the relative peace of the sixth-floor executive suite.

Here Seth would have no choice but to talk to her.

As if on cue, his office door opened. He strode out behind Gideon, his father and brother, who exchanged pleasantries with her, expressed sympathy for her ordeal and eventually got around to goodbye. Once they'd gone, she picked up her tea. It was cold.

Seth's brown gaze wasn't. Her body hummed in automatic response to his warm eyes.

"What are you doing here?"

"I work here." She busied herself shuffling a pile of perfectly stacked papers to prove it.

"You could have taken the day off."

"I've had three days off. Four if you count Friday. Plus a beautiful all-expenses-paid vacation to a tropical island."

He studied her as if he didn't understand sarcasm. "Look, Emma. About what happened. I'm sorry."

Her shoulders jerked involuntarily. She knew what was coming. Could hear it in his conciliatory tone. "About the shipwreck or the sex?"

"Both, I guess."

"That's too bad. I'm not particularly sorry about either one."

His chin fell to his chest. "Let's don't do this here. Come into my office and sit."

His office. Where he was king. "I'd prefer not to."

He raised his head. This time there was nothing remotely warm in his eyes.

Emma was plenty hot, though. The anger that had built up through long hours of the night spewed out like a geyser. "Don't I even get my second date?"

"What?"

"I keep your calendar, remember? I know where you go and whom you go with. You never take the same woman out more than twice. I can accept that. But since the island was technically one long date, I thought I'd have another shot yet. Maybe get a nice dinner out of it before you tucked tail and ran."

A muscle in the back of Seth's jaw ticked. Cold fury washed off him in waves while defiance burned in Emma's cheeks.

It took a few moments for him to collect himself, but when he spoke again his voice was very tight, very controlled. "I'll be keeping my own calendar from now on."

A nearly hysterical laugh escaped her. "And I won't be taking any more little sailing trips with you."

"Fine."

"Fine."

"We have an understanding, then."

"I guess we do." She flopped into her chair.

Seth turned toward his office, then peered back over his shoulder. "About this weekend. I want you to know I'm sorry for any…inconvenience it may have caused. And rest assured, you'll be compensated for your time."

Emma dribbled tea down the front of her cream silk blouse. She wanted to pitch the mug at him, but managed to restrain herself. Barely. "*Compensated?* You want to pay me for— Why, you—"

The chime above the elevator sounded. The doors slid open and a woman with a short skirt and long legs slithered across the room toward Seth in a look-at-me, hip-swinging gait.

"Seth, darling, it's been a long time." She air-kissed both his cheeks.

"How did you get up here, Bridget?"

"Now don't scold, dear. Your security guard remembers me, and I just had to come and see for myself that you were okay after your terrible accident."

Emma could have given the mystery-woman an earful about the so-called accident story Seth and his family had fed the press, but she kept her mouth shut.

Seth held his hands out to his sides. "I'm fine, as you can see."

Her gaze swept up and down the length of him appreciatively. "So I can."

She hooked her arm in his and turned them toward his office. "Now tell me all about it."

"I'm not giving you a story, Bridget."

Ugh, Emma thought. A reporter.

Bridget widened her eyes plaintively, but the hurt was as false as whatever she'd stuffed in her D-cup bra. "As close as we are, you think I'm just here to pump you for information?"

"We haven't been *close* in a long while."

Ah. A reporter *and* a victim of the two-date rule, Emma surmised.

"And I know you," Seth continued. "You're like a barracuda when it comes to the news. You don't know when to let go."

"Why, thank you, darling."

"You're welcome."

Seth subtly turned toward the elevator and strolled

forward. Bridget held him back when they reached Emma's desk.

"And this must be the brave young compatriot who faced death with you."

Seth looked like he wanted to drag Bridget to the elevator, but stopped short. "Emma Carpenter, meet Bridget Vaughn, columnist for the *Daily Envoy*."

Emma hadn't recognized the face, but she knew the name. From her political exposés to society gossip, Bridget Vaughn was famous for stirring up trouble in Emerald Cove's daily newspaper.

"Nice to meet you," Emma lied pleasantly.

"Since the big lug won't talk to me, can I beg, badger or bribe you into telling me what really happened out on that island?"

She met Seth's eyes over Bridget's shoulder for a moment. Oh, it was tempting. So tempting. But even angry at him as she was, she wouldn't stoop that low.

"I doubt it," she said.

Bridget shrugged. "Can't blame a girl for trying."

Seth nudged his ex-girlfriend toward the elevator. "I really have a full day. But it was nice seeing you again."

"Um-hmm," Bridget said, sauntering into the lift and turning around. "Not nearly as nice as it could have been."

She blew an air kiss at him as the door slid shut, and Emma's stomach turned.

As the lift hummed down six floors, Bridget Vaughn straightened her blouse, checked her lipstick in the chrome paneling and smiled wickedly.

There had been enough tension simmering between Seth and his castaway secretary to set off a fire alarm.

She didn't know what was going on between them, but whatever it was, it was explosive.

Emma Carpenter.

She committed the name to memory.

That one would bear watching.

Six

"You're going to miss your flight."

And Emma was going to go crazy if Seth didn't get out of the office soon. She couldn't take another of the cool, detached conversations that had become the norm since they'd returned from the island two weeks ago and reached their "agreement." Nor could she take any more of the looks he gave her between the conversations. Tortured looks that told her more than words ever could.

When he'd first refused to acknowledge his relationship with her, she thought he was simply a snob. A blue-blood CEO too genteel to be caught diddling his secretary. But as time passed and her emotions calmed, her opinion changed.

She didn't know what had happened to him in the past to cause him to entrench himself so firmly behind excuses like professionalism and ethics, to never date a woman more than twice, even if she didn't work for him.

What she did know was that those problems were his, not hers.

She had bigger issues on her mind.

Handing him his ticket, briefcase and copy of the *Daily Envoy* for airplane reading, she showed him to the elevator. If he didn't move, she was going to be late to her own appointment.

"Don't forget," he said, raking his hand through his hair and eliciting tingling memories of how that sleek brown hair had felt sliding through *her* fingers. "Mr. Petersen is faxing over his selections for the upholstery on his yacht. Get it over to my mother for a look-see so she can provide a little guidance if he's mixing purple curtains and leopard print bedspreads again."

"I'll handle it."

"The insurance adjuster is supposed to call with the final numbers on the *Strictly Business* loss. And don't forget—"

Emma threw up her hands. "Seth, you're only going to be gone one afternoon. The place won't fall apart."

Her exasperation took him back a second, then one corner of his mouth hooked briefly in what could have been a smile. It was the first sign of good humor she'd seen from him since the island.

"All right, then. I'll see you tomorrow. Looks like you've got everything under control."

Looks could be deceiving, but she didn't remind him of that. She was too busy trying not to fall apart until after he left.

"Have a good meeting," she said. As if that was possible. Seth hadn't told her why he was flying to Maryland, but Yankovich had. The navy was nervous about the security problems at Evans Yachts. They were afraid their multi million dollar submarine plans might fall into the wrong hands. They wanted assurances, and Seth was going to give them some.

Emma was just happy he was going to be out of the office for the day, no matter what the reason.

He nodded and stepped on the elevator, but hooked

the door with one broad palm before it could close. "You okay? You look a little pale."

Pale? Try weak-kneed. Numb. Terrified.

"I'm fine."

Though he didn't look convinced, he nodded good-bye once more and the elevator doors closed.

Thank goodness. Now she could fall apart.

She'd no sooner slumped in her chair than she noticed the numbers on the elevator display heading back up. Three...four...five...

The elevator chimed, but it wasn't Seth who stepped out when the doors whisked open. Emma gritted her teeth and plastered on a fake smile for her least-favorite member of the press. "Mr. Evans isn't in, Ms. Vaughn."

Without a glance toward Seth's office, Bridget sauntered across the room and propped her hip on Emma Carpenter's desk. "Oh, come now," she said, leaning across the desk. "After all the voice mails I've left you, you should be able to call me Bridget."

"There's a reason those phone calls weren't returned, Ms. Vaughn. I have nothing to say."

"You were stranded on a deserted island for three days with one rich, gorgeous hunk of a man. Honey, what you *don't* have to say every woman in Florida would like to read. In my column."

Emma stood and Bridget noticed the poor woman looked tired. Seth had a reputation as a slave driver, but this was ridiculous.

"I hate to be rude, Ms. Vaughn, but I need to lock the office up. Mr. Evans is out of town, and I have an appointment myself this afternoon."

How interesting. While the big bad bear was away, little cubby would play.

Bridget coughed violently, covering her mouth with one hand and clutching the other to her chest.

Emma blinked in concern. "Are you all right?"

Bridget carried on a little longer for good measure. "Let me get you some water."

As soon as Seth's secretary disappeared into the coffee room, Bridget flipped open the woman's date book—1:00 p.m. Emerald Cove Women's Health Center.

A card was stuck in the page. Dr. Susan Milton, OB-GYN.

How very, very interesting.

Bridget closed the date book seconds before Emma returned with the water. "Better," she said in a purposefully rough voice, then thanked Emma and said she'd be on her way.

She needed to see who she knew at the Emerald Cove Women's Health Center.

Seth was glad to be back in his own office, even if the navy had sicced Marcus on him to oversee security for Project Stingray. They'd insisted he fly down and supervise improvement personally. Even now Seth's adopted cousin sat across the desk from him, squinting at a set of blueprints.

"We'll put in card readers here, here, here and here," he said, thunking his pointer finger down on the desk.

"How long will that take?"

"Two days, max."

Seth shook his head. "Sorry to keep you away from your family that long."

"Samantha will deal. She always does." He looked up and grinned. "Besides, this way I might actually get some sleep. You've never seen a kid have to eat every hour the way little Henry—Hank, we're thinking about calling him—does.''

Actually, Seth had, but he didn't remind Marcus of it. That was a time best not thought about.

Marcus's smile fell. "I sure do miss the little pug, though. Kind of sneaks up on me, sometimes. Guess losin' a little sleep's not so bad, all things considered.''

"No, I guess not." Seth forced his mind to task. "So let's get this done and get you back to your family. What did you find out about this nutcase De-Bruzkya?''

Marcus straightened. "That he's not just a nutcase. He's got a pretty strong base in Rebelia, and now in Holzberg, or at least the disputed Peninsula of Sharfa. Intel says he's got a widespread espionage network feeding him information. Maybe even people here in the U.S.''

Surprise hummed through Seth. "You mean the bastard could be spying on us?''

Marcus hunched over his plans again. "Don't worry, cuz. I swept this room for bugs already.''

"Bugs?" Restlessness got the better of Seth and he left his desk to stand before the window, gazing out over the sugary beach and crystal blue waters. It was hard to believe foreign spies could operate in Emerald Cove. "Just how close do you think they are?" he asked quietly. "Do you think they could have planted the bomb on the *Strictly Business?*''

Marcus shoved back in his seat, stretched his massive body out. "Let's just say you should be taking different routes to and from work everyday. Vary your schedule.'' He grinned. ''And stay away from big glass windows.''

For the first time in his three years as CEO, Seth closed the vertical blinds in his office. ''What about Gideon?''

''He's being taken care of.''

Seth let the vague remark go. Gideon was Marcus's brother, and Marcus was nothing if not a fanatic about family. If he said the Faulkners' security was handled, it was handled.

He was about to question the adequacy of the building's alarm system when Holt blew into his office like a monsoon, their father on his heels. ''We got trouble, bro.''

Dread dropped like a stone in Seth's chest. Even Marcus looked worried. ''What? Another bomb?''

Holt plopped into a leather-tufted armchair and set his feet on the edge of Seth's desk. ''Worse. Mom's in a dither.''

''Damn it, Holt, you scared the hell out of me. Get your feet off my desk. For that matter, get out of my office.''

''Maybe you'd better give us a second, son.''

Seth lowered his voice to a respectful level. ''Pop, I have work.''

''It'll keep.'' The eldest Evans looked over his shoulder to the open office door. ''Where's your secretary?''

''Went downstairs to get the specs on the building's electrical systems for Marcus. Why?''

''You haven't read the morning paper, have you?''

The *Daily Envoy* sat folded untouched on the corner of his desk. ''Not yet.''

"Page seventeen. Society column," Holt said cheekily.

Seth snatched up the paper and thumbed through until he found the page.

WILD ISLAND TIMES?

Miss Emma Carpenter, twenty-six-year-old executive assistant to local CEO Seth Evans, is carrying her first child. The conception date? Approximately two weeks ago, right about the time she and Mr. Evans were marooned together for three days on an uninhabited island off Key—

"Pregnant!"

Seth glared at the empty desk in the outer office, then grabbed the phone and punched in seven numbers from memory. His hand gripped the phone so tightly he thought he might break the casing while the line rang once. Twice.

"What the hell kind of trash is this you're printing?" he growled without preamble when Bridget picked up.

"It's not trash."

But it wasn't Bridget who had spoken.

Emma stood in his door, a folder clutched against her chest, her vivid green eyes glimmery and her lashes wet. Red flags unfurled on her pale cheeks.

Seth hung up the phone.

Emma swallowed hard. Her shoulders straightened. "I'm going to have a baby."

The English maiden held her head high as her Viking captor marched her down the flimsy plank toward—

A chair.

"Sit, Emma," Seth ordered, snapping her back to reality.

Her head hung. She felt more like a child in the principal's office than a brave English maid.

Seth paced the confines of his office. Marcus, Holt and his father had excused themselves. Quickly.

Emma wished she could have sneaked out behind them.

"How the hell did this happen?" he asked, then pinched the bridge of his nose. "Never mind. I know how it happened. Why didn't you tell me? I had to read it in the damn newspaper?"

"I just found out for sure myself yesterday. I don't know how Ms. Vaughn found out so soon."

He sighed. "It's a talent she has."

"I was going to tell you. Today. I was just working up how."

He stopped pacing on the far side of the room, shoved his hands in his pockets and rattled change. She studied his broad back, watched the muscles ripple beneath his shirt as she waited.

"Do you want a child, Emma?" he finally asked.

"Would I want to get pregnant if I weren't already? No. But now that I am, I don't see that it matters whether I want one or not. I'm having a baby. Any other option isn't an option for me."

He had the good grace to look relieved at that, at least. "Then you'll keep it?"

"Of course." Even if she had to give up all her goals, all her dreams, to do it.

"It's not easy to raise a child alone."

"I'll make do."

He stared into space as if critiquing a classic piece

of art. She'd learned to recognize that look over the months. Seth Evans in full CEO mode. Wheels turning. Evaluating alternatives. When he rolled his shoulders, she knew he'd come to a decision.

"I can't let you do it," he said.

He might as well have kicked her in the chest. "I don't think you can stop me." She laid her hand over the belly that was still flat, but wouldn't be for long. "Or him or her."

"I can't let you raise my child alone."

Indignation raised the short hairs on the back of her neck. "*Our* child."

He leaned over her. "I won't be relegated to playing father every other weekend and a month during summer vacation."

"Seth, you're getting a little ahead of yourself."

"Am I? Or are you already way ahead of me?"

"What are you talking about?"

"How long ago did you think through all this? All the way back on the island? You know me well enough to know I wouldn't turn my back on a child. My child."

Her lip curled. "You think I purposely got pregnant? To what—trap you?"

He stood stone silent.

"I suppose if you hadn't been the one to insist I go sailing with you, you'd think I was the one who set the bomb on the boat, too, just to get us stranded and nudge you in the right direction. Maybe I conjured the storm to move things along. Bewitched you into saying—" She bit back her tears. She would *not* cry. "Into saying that you wanted me."

Inscrutable, he folded his arms over his chest.

She rose to leave. She'd had enough.

He hooked her elbow and stopped her. "If you think I'm going to get down on one knee and beg, think again."

He'd gone stark, raving insane. There was no other explanation. "Let me go."

"Marry me, Emma. That's the best offer you're going to get."

The walls closed in around her. "You've lost your mind. Let me go."

He held fast. "If I'm going to have a child, by God I'm going to be a father to it. I have that right."

Emma's heart skittered like a scared rabbit. He did have that right. How many men had it and threw it away? And here he was fighting for it. Fighting for his child.

A child she couldn't deny him.

That still didn't mean she could marry him, though. "I—I can't."

"Why not?" His brown eyes were dark. Dangerous.

Because she was the one who would be trapped, then. She'd be stuck in a loveless, passionless existence without respite or escape. Living an existence as cold and useless as a marble statue in his fancy home somewhere. She'd be nothing more than an adornment—and a plain one at that—in his fancy life. An afterthought he kept around to swaddle his child.

That wasn't the future she wanted. For herself or her child.

"Don't fight me on this," he said, squeezing her arm painfully. "That's *my* baby you're carrying."

She couldn't marry Seth. It was crazy.

Yet she couldn't deny him his child, either.

Emma needed to get away. Needed to think. She jerked her arm from his grasp. "I need some time."

Seth released her. "Sure, doll. Take all the time you want."

He called to her as she rushed out the door. Against her better judgment she stopped, turned, met his polished stone eyes.

"As long as I have my answer by 8:00 a.m. tomorrow," he finished flatly. "Not a minute after."

Seven

Emma expected Yankovich to fire her. Remove her from the assignment at the very least. She'd failed miserably. Made a horrible, embarrassing, life-altering mess of everything.

And yet there was one good thing to come out of it. She laid her hand across her abdomen. One precious gift.

"You saw the newspaper?" she asked when it was her turn at the counter in the dry cleaner, and the rest of the customers had left. Her cheeks flamed.

Yankovich bit the end off a cigar and spit it in the wastebasket. "I saw."

"I'm prepared for whatever consequences you see fit. I—"

"How did Evans take it?"

She thought about lying, but saw no point.

"Not well."

"He dump you?"

Her shoulders ached with the effort of holding them square when she wanted so badly to crumble. "He asked me to marry him. Actually, he pretty much insisted on it."

"And you agreed?"

Crusty old bugger, Emma thought. He asked the question with no more empathy than he might ask if she'd changed the oil in her car last month. "No."

"Why not?"

She faltered, taken too off guard to be angry. "I—I hardly know him."

He stared pointedly at her midsection. "Know him well enough, I'd say."

Now she was angry. Nothing that had happened between her and Seth was sleazy or ugly. It had been...extraordinary. Full of passion. Full of life. She refused to regret a moment of it.

Even if Seth regretted *every* moment of it.

She jutted her chin in the air. "I assume you'll want a new operative in place as soon as possible. I'll be resigning from Evans Yachts today. I'll wait your further instructions from home." She about-faced and headed for the exit.

"Whoa, whoa. Hold on, there." Yankovich dodged around the end of the counter and blocked her way, his back to the door, arms spread defensively. "Let's just think on this a minute."

Grudgingly, she stopped. She wasn't going to get in a physical confrontation with him. The fact that he was her boss aside, the man was built like a bulldog.

He squinted at her. "You're in love with him, aren't you?"

To her horror, tears pooled around the rims of her eyes.

"Aw, now, dry your decks, missy." He took her by the elbow with surprising gentleness and led her back to the counter.

A man entered with an armload of suits on hangers. Emma pulled herself together while Yankovich served him.

Spies did not cry.

When the customer left, Yankovich flipped the sign

on the door to Closed and pulled her to the back of the store.

She sat in the hard wooden chair he gestured toward. Knees pinned together and hands twisting in her lap, she said, "I'm sorry this situation has gotten so complicated."

"Yeah, well. Life's complicated."

So she was learning.

The vinyl covering on his chair squeaked beneath his bulk when he sat and propped his feet up.

With no clear understanding why he'd brought her back here—unless it was so he could chew her out without interruption—Emma waited.

He considered her across the desk. "Won't be easy to get someone new close to Evans."

Good, she wanted to say, but held her tongue. He might be a moron when it came to women—especially pregnant women—but Seth was a decent, honest person. He didn't deserve to be deceived.

"I'm sure you'll find a way. You have resources—"

"Maybe you should reconsider."

She tilted her head. "Resigning?"

"Marrying him."

Heat swam to her cheeks. "That's not possible."

"Man's trying to do the right thing. Why not give him a chance?"

"Because he doesn't want me," she blurted, wishing she could take the words back even before the last one left her mouth.

"You sure of that?"

She nodded.

"Sometimes things happen too fast, a man loses his

bearings. Takes him awhile to get back on course. Could be you're abandoning ship too soon.''

Emma reflected on the hard look in Seth's eyes when he'd found out she was pregnant. She couldn't see him changing his mind. Ever.

''I appreciate your...concern, sir. But this is something I have to work out on my own.''

His feet clomped to the floor. ''All right. Then look at it this way. I need information. You have a chance to get closer to Seth Evans than anyone's ever been.''

Emma nearly choked. ''Surely you can't mean you want me to accept his proposal just so I can continue my surveillance.''

''And if I told you I can, and do?''

Emma stood. ''I'd tell you to go to hell.''

To her surprise, Yankovich laughed. ''I can see why Evans likes you. You've got grit.''

She wasn't so sure Evans *did* like her.

Yankovich's weary eyes gentled. ''What are you going to do? Run back to Iowa? Find a string of pig farmers to take care of you, like your mother?''

He knew just where to hit her. She loved her parents. Her mother had raised her with a gentle hand and her father never neglected her, even after the divorce. But as her parents had divorced and remarried time and again, she'd been bounced from home to home. Family to family. At times, when her newest stepmother or stepfather wasn't so fond of kids, she'd been packed off to uncles and aunts. Dropped on their doorsteps like an unwanted kitten.

Eventually she'd learned to stay in whatever room she was assigned, stay quiet. Maybe if they forgot she was there, they wouldn't send her away again.

It was in one of those rooms that she'd first begun

to daydream. To escape her bland existence in storybook tales of excitement and adventure where she was dashing, daring and in control. Well, not always in control, like the pirate dream. But everything always worked out in the end.

But would a life with Seth work out in the end? Or would she be just another unwanted burden?

And what about her child?

"I don't know what I'm going to do," she admitted honestly.

"Then maybe you shouldn't be in such a rush to turn down Evans's proposal. There's a lot at stake here."

Yankovich grunted and flopped back in his chair. "For both of us."

Seth walked through the cavernous boat works attached behind the Evans Yachts office building, his hands in his pockets and the leather soles of his wingtips scuffing the cement floor. On his left, shelves of rolled fiberglass rose from floor to lofty ceiling. On his right, hollow boat molds sat uncovered, ready for pouring. And in the center, resting in special lifts like babes in their cradles, a motor yacht and two sailboats waited finishing.

It was after six in the evening, so the workers had gone for the day, but the acrid scent of resin still tinged the air and there was a vibrancy in the hum of fluorescent lights overhead, the low whistle of the air ventilators. An excitement. As if the building itself anticipated their return.

Seth didn't get down to the assembly area as often as his father had. Russ liked to work with his hands, often decking out in a clean suit to spray gelcoat, or going over a hull section with a hand roller, inch by painstaking inch, to squeeze out any air trapped between the layers of laminate.

Seth preferred the business end of building boats. The intellectual challenge of making the numbers work, negotiating deals with suppliers and buyers.

But the factory was really the center of it all, the heart of the company that had sustained three generations of Evanses across seven decades. Tonight Seth needed to feel the connection with his family's lifeblood. His history and his legacy.

A legacy he hoped to pass on to his own child someday.

The possibility that he could end up little more than an afterthought in his child's life, not have a say in how he or she was raised, the values that were formed, bore down on Seth like the strain on the mast of an overcanvased boat in a heavy wind. Sighing, he propped himself against an unfinished hull.

"'Bout time you dragged your butt out of that pretty office of yours and got down here to see firsthand what kind of business you're running."

Seth jolted upright. His father stepped from behind the sailboat-in-the-making.

"Pop. I thought everyone was gone."

"Everyone but me." He strolled toward Seth. "Tried to call you a few times this afternoon. Rolled to voice mail."

"I had a full schedule and—" His jaw hardened. "Emma went home early."

"You had your talk with her, I take it?"

He nodded once. Sharply.

"And?"

"It didn't go well."

Pop gave him a long, appraising look. Seth didn't doubt that his father could read every crease of tension in his face, every bunched muscle in his shoulders, despite his outwardly casual stance. Pop knew him too well. Just like he knew Seth didn't like to talk about personal matters. Especially personal matters that involved disastrous relationships with women.

Abruptly, the elder Evans looked away. "This Holt's boat for the regatta?"

Knowing he wasn't off the hook—his dad sometimes had a roundabout way of getting to a conversation, but he always got there—Seth nodded.

"You've changed the keel some." His dad ran a hand over the hull of the *Unicorn*, feeling for imperfections.

He wouldn't find any. Seth had personally made sure of it. He might rag his brother about his racing addiction, but he wouldn't let Holt go out in anything but the best. "Computer modeled it at five percent less drag."

His father's eyebrows lifted. "Five? You're gonna make your brother a happy man."

Seth snorted, a grin crooking one corner of his mouth. "Give Holt a leaky dinghy and a bed sheet for a sail and he's a happy man. So long as he can be on the water. What I'm hoping to make him is a winner."

"I'm sure he appreciates that. What about you, Seth?"

Seth looked up, not following.

"What does it take to make you happy?"

The margin of relaxation he'd found slipped away. "I've got everything I want." The company. His work. A BMW Z3 convertible.

"Everything?"

Giving in to the inevitability of this conversation, he sighed. "I already asked her to marry me, Pop."

"She said no?"

"Rather vehemently."

His father strolled off, inspecting Holt's boat again. "Look at this beauty, the craftsmanship. She's a real work of art." He caressed her bow like a lover's breast. "What do you suppose would happen if we'd hacked out her hull with a jackhammer and pounded on her deck with two-penny nails?"

"I suppose she'd sink. Is there a point to this?"

"If a man wants to build something to last—including a relationship—he can't do it with brute force. It takes finesse."

"You accusing me of being heavy-handed?"

"Not physically. We both know you're a better man than that. But given your history—"

Seth flinched. He'd been trying to avoid comparing this situation to what had happened with Tiffany.

"—and the frame of mind you were in after you read that newspaper article, I doubt you handled this situation with kid gloves."

Seth frowned. He hadn't been any harder on Emma than he'd been on himself.

"You care about this woman, son?"

Did he? He'd worked with Emma for six months. He was attracted to her. More, he liked her. Respected her. And as much as he tried to deny it, he cared about her on a personal level. She was pretty, smart and gutsy. She could be funny when she wanted to be, serious when it was called for.

And she was carrying his child.

His stomach flipped over. "Yeah. Yeah, I care

about her.'' But that hadn't stopped him from mucking things up.

His father grinned. ''Then what are you doing hanging around a musty old factory on a Friday night?''

''I don't know, Pop.'' He clapped his old man on the back. ''What do you say we both get out of here?''

Seth checked his watch. It was early yet. Plenty of time to make a few stops downtown before he knocked on Emma's door and set things right.

A rivulet of chilly water from her damp hair dribbled down Emma's neck and ran between her shoulder blades. She sat in an overstuffed chair printed with lilacs, bare feet tucked beneath her, clutched the collar of her chenille robe tighter around her throat and sipped a mug of spearmint tea. She needed the tea. She'd spent twenty minutes under a steaming shower and still her nerves hadn't settled.

The confrontation this morning with Seth, and then another this afternoon with Yankovich, not to mention her own anxieties, had her jumping at shadows.

With the remote control she switched on a mellow jazz CD. The music unwound her, until the door buzzer scratched through the crooning sax. Jolted upright, she sloshed hot tea over her hand and nearly dropped the mug.

Grabbing the napkin she'd set over the coaster and dabbing up the mess, she yelled, ''Just a second.''

It was a full forty-five seconds before she pulled the door open. The scents of sandalwood cologne and fresh flowers greeted her. Seth seemed to be the source of both.

He smiled across the threshold at her, his hair

combed, jaw clean-shaven and holding a handful of yellow tulips in florist's paper.

Emma stared at him. Gaped, actually.

"Can I come in?"

She clutched her robe to her throat. "What are you doing here?"

"Apologizing, if you'll let me."

She hesitated only a moment before swinging the door open and walking away. It clicked shut behind her, ominously loud against the hushed music.

"Not necessary," she said.

When his broad hand landed on her shoulder, she jumped again. She hadn't heard him come up behind her.

"I think it is."

She turned under his urging hand and realized instantly it was a mistake when his cool brown gaze plunged right through her. Hooked, she dangled like a fish on a line.

"I...handled things badly this morning."

She hardly felt it when he put the flowers in her numb hands. "Uh-huh."

Lovely. How eloquent.

"I'm hoping to do better the second time around."

He let go of her shoulders and she stepped back, suddenly released from his spell. Needing time, distance, she made an excuse about putting the flowers in water, then retreated to her bedroom to put on some clothes and brush out her hair. When she returned, it was he who gave her his back. He stood staring out her balcony window. The breadth of his shoulders blocked her view, but she knew the lights would be twinkling, glittering off the water.

"Not as pretty as the view from your condo, I bet," she said.

He looked a moment longer, then turned. "It's nice." His gaze roamed the postage-stamp-sized living room with its well-worn, overstuffed furniture, the handwoven tapestries hung on the walls in place of paintings, the whimsical multicolored paper butterflies that hung over the dining room table. "It suits you."

A slow warmth suffused her cheeks. The flattery was nice, but what did he really want here?

"Look, the flowers are thoughtful, but nothing has cha—"

"You accused me once of holding out on you. You were right." He paced across her beige carpeting like a savvy gator stalking a skittish heron. "You're still right."

He stopped in front of her, close. Instinct screamed for her to take a step back, but she fought it. She was through stepping back from him.

"What are you holding back now?"

"Do you really want a baby, Emma? Have you really thought it through?"

"I think we had this conversation already."

"No." He stopped, looked at her again with that intensity burning in his eyes that kept her from looking away. "I mean do you *want* a baby? Ever. A son or daughter to tuck in at night, to pick up from school and take to soccer practice and karate class and dance school during the day? To teach all the things you've learned and keep from making all the mistakes you made?"

"I—I guess." The enormity of what was happening to her, growing in her belly, stirred deep inside her. "I never thought much—"

"I have," Seth answered without letting her finish. She'd never heard such emotion, raw and uncontrolled, in two simple words. "I've wanted a child for years. Since I...dated a woman who had a son. I...got close to him. Too close."

He paused, struggling with demons she couldn't see or understand.

Is this what he hadn't told her? "What happened?"

He shrugged stiffly. "Things didn't work out between us. She moved out of town, took Josh with her. I tried to contact her but—"

He raked the hair from his face. The pain in his haggard eyes moved her more than any words he could have said. In all the times she'd looked at him, seen the CEO, the mark, the man, she'd missed the one thing he really wanted to be.

A father.

"You never saw him again?"

"Never." He dragged in a deep breath. "Made me realize, though, how much I liked being a dad."

"This was a long time ago?" she guessed.

"Nearly ten years."

Surprise tumbled through her. "Ten years? You could have had children of your own by now, but you've never married."

"Things ended badly between Josh's mom and me. So badly that I wasn't sure I ever wanted to get that deep into a relationship again." The energy that had pulsed around him when he talked about having a child went silent. "One of life's little ironies, don't you think? That I can't have the child I want without being saddled with a woman, too."

She wheeled, a sudden spurt of anger gushing from

deep inside. Without even trying, it scraped at an open wound. Made her bleed.

She didn't want to be anybody's burden.

"Biology is a bitch, isn't it?" she said, but before she could stomp away, his hands were on her again, turning her.

"Emma. I didn't mean you. I just—"

It wasn't like him to stumble over his words. She waited while he collected himself, too curious to turn away.

"I haven't had such good experiences with women. I guess I'm a little gun shy. But I wanted you to understand why it's so important to me that you marry me."

His hands sent tingling messages through her shoulders. Gradually, her muscles relaxed, her flight instinct died. "So that you can have your child."

He nodded.

"You don't have to marry me for that. I wouldn't take your child away from you."

She couldn't, now that she knew.

"I can't take that risk." He lifted her chin with one hand, wound his other in her hair behind her head and pulled her close, millimeter by millimeter. Their hips collided, then their chests. His heat seeped through her T-shirt, and she briefly wished she still wore her robe. Without it, she felt every contour of his broad chest, his slabbed belly. And she knew he felt every contour of her, as well. Including the way her nipples peaked and her breath hitched at his nearness.

"It wouldn't be so bad, Emma," he murmured, his mouth inches from hers. "You and me."

Emma could no more pull away from him than the tide could pull away from the moon. Panic swelled inside her at the control he had over her. "But we don't love each other."

"We felt something for each other. On the island."

"That was...different."

"Okay. Then tell me you never thought about this before the island." He touched the tip of his tongue to her earlobe and drew a line down to the pulse point at the base of her neck, drawing a shiver out of her.

She'd be lying if she did.

"Or this." His hips lapped at hers like waves against the shore, and she felt the beginnings of his arousal.

"Or this." His mouth found hers. His tongue fondled the crease between her lips while his hand in her hair dragged her head back, giving him better access. The night exploded around her in a white-hot barrage of heat and light and her knees went weak.

She should push him away, slap him. But he was the only thing holding her up, so instead she leaned against him, felt his heart bang against hers.

A moment later, he intensified the kiss. Then, tearing himself away, he righted her with hands under both her elbows, and when she was steady, stalked as far away from her as he could get in the tiny apartment.

"Damn it." He shook his head and shoved his hands in the pockets of his pressed Dockers, looking at her out of ravaged eyes. "That's not why I came here, Emma. I swear."

She collected herself and managed to get to her overstuffed chair, where she sat before she fell. "Why *did* you come here?"

He dug around in his pocket and pulled out a small

box. He came over to her chair, sat on the arm and opened it.

A perfect princess-cut diamond on a white-gold band winked up at her, two carats, at least.

"I came to bring you this and to ask you—beg you, if I have to—to marry me."

She took the ring from its velvet bed and turned it over in her hand, watching the light bounce off the facets, then raised her head sadly. "You mean to sell myself—and my child—to you."

"No," he said, low and urgent. "I mean share yourself and our child with me."

He took hold of her hand, linked his fingers with hers and rested them on her abdomen. "I want to be a part of this little life. I want to be there for it. Every morning. Every night. Not a part-time dad."

He drew a deep breath, took the ring from her and lifted her left hand. "This is my baby, too," he said, slowly sliding the band over her first knuckle. "I have a right to be a father to it. Don't deny me that right. Please."

Tears gathered in Emma's eyes as she realized he was right. She couldn't deny him his own child. "No," she said, and the first teardrop fell. "I won't."

Even if it meant becoming that which she most despised.

Someone else's burden.

But before she could marry him, she had to tell him the truth about who she was and why she was here.

Seth slid the ring home, to the base of her finger.

All other thoughts crashed around her, wiped away like a sandcastle by the rising surf.

A sea breeze played in the pale maiden's hair, drying her tears as she cried alone, always alone, a pris-

oner on the balcony of the ivory tower condo by the sea, slowly fading away while below, her dream lover and his child romped in the sand—

A pair of warm lips pulled her from the daydream, kissing away the trail of her tears from her eyelashes over her cheek to the corner of her mouth. He nibbled there, coaxing.

She opened her eyes, met the liquid amber in his brown gaze. Her heart thrummed like a symphony percussion section. "Seth, there's something I have to tell—"

"Emma," he groaned, slanting his mouth over hers and then plunging into her. "Don't cry. Please don't cry."

She forgot what she needed so desperately to say and opened to him. For a moment that felt like a lifetime, their tongues danced. His hands fisted in her hair and hers in his shirt. With a supreme will, she gathered the strength to push against him. She had to tell him.

"Seth, we've got to talk—"

He staggered backward, raking one hand through his hair. "I know. I'm sorry. Just because we're getting married doesn't mean I expect— I mean you don't have to—"

He blew out an explosive breath. "Ah, hell. Sleeping with me isn't part of the deal if you don't want it to be. I thought we could take things slow. Get to know each other in the more traditional way. Then if something…I don't know…happened, great. If not, I understand."

She shook her head, trying to follow what he was saying. "Seth, you're rambling."

"Yeah." A crooked grin creased his face. "Odd, isn't it?"

He looked at her with such fire burning beneath his molten gold eyes that she thought he might stomp right back across the room and kiss her again. But instead he opened the door behind him, already bowing out.

"Good night, Emma."

He was gone before she got a chance to tell him that the woman who'd just agreed to marry him wasn't who he thought she was.

Eight

"Seth tells us you're from Maryland, Emma."

Emma watched as Seth's mother, Lynn, set her crystal wine goblet on the long cherry dining table and took her seat at the corner near where his father sat at the head of the table.

"And Iowa," Seth added, pushing in Emma's chair and taking the one next to it. Marcus, Drew, Holt, Seth's sister Laura, Gideon and his wife Brooke all looked at her expectantly from their places around the table.

She felt like a bug under a microscope.

Seth anticipated her uneasiness. He laid a calming hand on her shoulder. "Her family has a farm there."

"Really? What kind of farm?"

"Pigs mostly. I—I just spent summers there," she added, shamed at how easily the lie rolled off her tongue. Like circles in the water when a stone plopped in, lies always seemed to get bigger. The ripple effect.

She should have already straightened things out with Seth, but he hadn't given her a chance. He'd left suddenly Friday night, then hadn't come by at all on Saturday. She supposed he'd been working, as he usually did. He never asked her to put in the overtime, but she could always tell Monday morning that he'd been there. The desk she'd left clean Friday evening was stacked with memos to be sent, folders to be filed, materials to be ordered.

He had sent her another bouquet of flowers, though. Roses this time, with a card that read: Family dinner tonight at 7:00. I'll pick you up. Please let me know if you can't make it.

She supposed she should have been insulted that he hadn't asked her in person. Then again, after what had happened between them Friday night, maybe he was afraid to be alone with her.

Plus, she got the feeling he was trying to give her some space, which she appreciated. Soon she had to tell him the truth, though, regardless of the circumstances. Before the lies got any further out of hand.

"Emma?"

Emma looked up, lost.

Seth squeezed her hand beneath the table. "Mom was asking if we'd set a date yet."

"A date?"

Seth laughed. The others around the table smiled bemusedly.

"A date for the wedding, honey."

Heat rushed to Emma's cheeks. "Oh. Well, we, uh, haven't really talked about it yet." But she was wearing his ring.

Seth held her gaze. "Soon, though. We were thinking soon."

Emma's chest constricted as she wondered just *how* soon. How many days left before she gave up her independence. Dropped herself on Seth's doorstep the way she'd been dropped on aunts and uncles as a child.

Mrs. Evans beamed. Her eyes glistened, just a bit too full. Her husband, Seth's father, Russell, touched her arm, leaned over and brushed her cheek with a kiss. She leaned her head on his shoulder a moment, then straightened.

How different their marriage was than her parents' had been, Emma thought. She'd forgotten that kind of love still existed.

She cleared the lump from her throat and scanned the table. "Drew, I know you're a pilot, and Marcus, you're in the navy."

She avoided making eye contact with Marcus, afraid she'd give away exactly how much she knew about Marcus and his navy assignment.

Or that he'd give away how much he knew about her.

Out of the corner of her eye, she caught him staring at her and felt a warning trill deep in her bones. "Laura," she continued, trying to seem unaffected, "I understand you're a marine biologist."

Holt leaned over and jabbed his sister in the ribs playfully. "Yep. She'd rather swim around with the fishes all day than work a real job with the family business."

Laura snapped her head up and toward her brother, swirling her chin-length brown hair around her face. "Oh, yeah. Like yacht racing is a *real* job."

"More real than studying seaweed."

Laura banged her fork down on her china plate. "Reefs. I study coral reefs."

"Hey, lighten up, you two," Seth interjected. "This is supposed to be a dinner party, not *Family Feud*."

"Don't let them bother you, dear," Mrs. Evans said, passing the steamed asparagus around the table. "You know how siblings are."

Actually, she didn't, being an only child. This

whole setting—the family dinner, the ribbing and the displays of affection—was as foreign to her as a moonscape. Foreign, and yet somehow…nice.

Watching Gideon Faulkner's expressions, she got the feeling he felt the same way. When he could take his eyes off of Brooke, that was.

What a beautiful couple the two of them made. Another love match.

Which made her feel the lack of love in her own engagement even more keenly.

She didn't fit into this family. Didn't feel a part of it.

Emma had been so nervous about meeting Seth's mother—as more than his secretary—that she'd had to ask him to pull his car over twice on the way here to settle her stomach. She'd agonized over whether Lynn would think her good enough for her son. Whether she would think Emma had trapped him. She never thought she'd be able to sit and make pleasant conversation all evening, much less eat.

Despite the fact that she'd learned yesterday that Emma was carrying her son's baby out of wedlock, Mrs. Evans was the perfect host, gracious as any First Lady. The whole family was warm and inviting—except Marcus. And before long she found herself not only eating, but enjoying herself.

Mrs. Evans smoothed a linen napkin in her lap. "Seth, has there been any more news about who might have broken into your office?"

The air around the table changed subtly, but noticeably. The men shared a look. It was brief, but unmistakable. Seth turned and shared it with her a moment, as if asking her to cooperate, and then answered his mother.

"Aw, it was probably just one of the racers trying to get a look at Holt's fancy new boat."

Holt nodded too enthusiastically. "We're going to have to drape her to hide that new keel design when we portage her out to the water."

With that, they slid neatly into a conversation about boats and keel designs and water speed records, avoiding any further discussions about the break-in at Evans Yachts. Interesting that Lynn didn't seem to know about the bomb.

Emma followed the ebb and flow of the conversation, wondering why Seth hadn't told the whole family the truth, but mostly she was aware of Marcus scrutinizing her from across the table. Coming from six-foot-something and about two tons of hard, muscled male, it was an uncomfortable scrutiny. Marcus was a Navy SEAL, a trained operative. Some would say a trained killer.

And the way he was looking at her right then, she would believe them.

She rubbed her hands over the goose bumps rising on her arms.

While the others talked on, Seth touched her shoulder. "Cold?"

She tried for a nonchalant smile. "I'm fine."

"You don't look it." His gaze traveled up the table. It was almost as though he followed the thread of energy hanging between her and Marcus. He frowned at his cousin, the two of them locking gazes for a moment like bulls locking horns.

Surprisingly, Marcus turned away first.

"Don't worry about him," Seth said quietly. "He might be built like The Incredible Hulk, but he's relatively harmless."

Harmless. Right.

She nodded weakly at Seth, not believing it for a minute, but not able to tell him.

When the meal ended, the women, including Emma, retired to the kitchen, but not without a warning glare at the men from Mrs. Evans first.

"One of you men leaves this area before your plate is rinsed and in the kitchen sink," she said, "you're dead meat."

In less than two minutes, a stack of clean plates slid into the soapy water. Emma was impressed.

While they cleared off the table, Emma chitchatted with Laura, who seemed to be almost as much an outsider in the Evans family as Emma. They didn't approve of her career choice, Emma gathered.

She could relate to that. Boy, could she relate. Her parents had not exactly been ecstatic over her life choices, either. They'd expected her to stay in Iowa, marry a farmer. To them, her chosen path must have seemed as far away as the moon.

That was what Emma had liked about it.

Once the chores were done, and with the men still nowhere in sight, Emma wandered out onto the patio. Sculpted hedges and ferns in stone planters the size of Volkswagens lined the multilevel redbrick terrace. A kidney-shaped swimming pool dove through the middle, with a hot tub beneath a very natural-looking waterfall that tinkled at one end. Great palm trees shot to the sky, their sparse fronds wavering in a light breeze above the tile roof of the main house. Below the lowest level of the terrace, the waterfront stretched as far as she could see in either direction.

Dusk crept up on the day, and the view took her breath away. The setting sun had turned the ocean surface to liquid gold. A magnificent yacht cruised the horizon under full sail.

She'd just sat on a stone bench to watch, listening to the slap of waves against the beach, when a hand clamped around her upper arm from behind her and Marcus growled, "What the hell do you think you're doing?"

In the billiards room, Russell Evans poured two fingers of Scotch into four glasses and handed them around. "How much does Emma know about Stingray?"

Seth downed his drink in one gulp. "Enough."

"You're going to have to tell her to zip it up around Mom and Laura." Holt took a sip of alcohol and wrinkled his nose.

"She's not stupid. She figured out what was going on."

Drew flopped into a leather armchair. "Seems to me that Seth here is the one who needs to learn to keep it zipped up."

Seth glared at him over the top of his empty glass.

"Don't be crude, Drew," Russ said.

Drew's grin fell. "Aw, don't get me wrong. She's a nice enough girl." He waggled his eyebrows at Holt. "Pretty enough, too. You should have seen her on that island wearing nothing but—"

"Boys!" Russell banged his glass down on an end table. "Do you mind?"

"Come on, Pop," Holt complained. "What's the fun of having a big brother get engaged if we can't give him a little crap over it?"

"Give him crap later. Right now we need to talk."

Holt downed his Scotch, trying to look sulky but hardly putting a dent in his perpetual good humor.

"How's security coming?" Seth's father asked.

Holt saluted. "All quiet on the home front, sir."

He turned to Seth. "The office?"

"Everything's in place. The Stingray documentation is locked down tight."

Russ nodded, scanned the room. "Where's Gideon?"

"Downstairs with the women," Seth answered. "Can't pry him away from his wife."

"Ain't that sweet," Holt chided.

"Leave him be, Holt," Russ said. He looked to Seth. "I assume he's secure?"

"I was hoping Marcus would move him into one of our offices this month so we'd all be closer, but Gideon prefers to work from home, and Marcus thought it would be better if we keep him tucked away where he is for the moment. Where'd Marcus go, anyway?"

No one seemed sure, and Seth didn't like that. He especially didn't like the vibes he'd been getting from Marcus all through dinner. Made him wonder what his cousin was up to.

Restless, he stood at the window over the terrace.

"Probably going back for fourths on the bouillabaisse," Holt joked. "What about the regatta? Do you think it's safe to bring the navy brass here?"

"I don't see that we have much choice. They aren't going to keep funding us without seeing their prototype, and the regatta is the best cover we're going to get for bringing a boatload of strangers into town without drawing attention to ourselves," his father said. "What do you think, Seth?"

"Hmm?" He'd been focused on the two figures

outlined beneath the watery light of a garden lantern outside.

"He said the Martians have landed and they've taken Emma," Holt said.

"Right." The two figures below moved closer. One reached out to the other. The smaller of the two figures turned. Seth caught a flash of kinky auburn hair in the lamplight. Emma started to walk away, but the bigger figure pulled her back forcibly.

Seth was halfway down the stairs before he drew his next breath.

Emma twisted in Marcus's grasp. "I said let me go, you big brute."

"And I asked what the hell kind of game you're playing with Seth."

Emma turned in his grasp and lifted her leg, ready to stomp down on Marcus's instep, but she didn't have to. Seth stepped out of the darkness, fists clenched at his sides and eyes blazing. "Take your hands off her or you're a dead man."

"Whoa, there, cousin—"

Seth landed two palms flat on Marcus's chest. The shove should have knocked the bigger man backward, but Marcus stood like a rock. Emma was the one who stumbled.

"I said let her go," Seth repeated. "Now."

"This isn't what it looks like."

Seth pulled back a fist.

Marcus narrowed his eyes. "You're kidding, right? You wouldn't land a single punch."

Emma didn't doubt that, given the man's genetically engineered strength.

"Maybe not," Seth growled, "but I'd get a lot of satisfaction out of trying."

Marcus rolled his eyes and raised his hands, releasing Emma.

"Go in the house, Em," Seth told her.

She glanced nervously from one man to the other. This whole thing was her fault. "It was just a misunderstanding, Seth. Please, let's both go inside. I'll explain everything later."

"Why don't you explain it to him now," Marcus taunted.

Emma's stomach tumbled. The lies were closing in on her.

"Marcus, please. This isn't the way. Now isn't the time."

"When is the time? Right after the wedding?"

Blood trickled through her veins on a thready pulse. "No. Just not here. Not like this."

"Will one of you tell me what the hell you're talking about?"

They both turned to Seth, who looked from one to the other of them as if they were both insane.

Marcus lowered his gaze to hers and shook his head. "You don't know what he's been through. How other women have lied to him. You don't have a clue what this is gonna do to him."

"Hello." Seth waved at them. "I'm standing right here. I'd appreciate if you didn't talk about me like I wasn't."

Emma ignored him, her mind still turning over what Marcus had said. Who had lied to Seth? Did it have something to do with the little boy he hadn't seen in a decade?

"I don't want to hurt him."

"Then tell him now. Bad news only gets worse with time."

"Tell me what?"

Emma and Marcus exchanged a long look, and finally she nodded reluctantly.

"Who she really is," Marcus said in a gentle voice that belied the power coiled in those massive muscles of his.

Seth searched her eyes, waiting. "Who?"

Emma gave up the fight. She had to do it now. Neither Marcus nor Seth would let her walk away until she'd spilled all her secrets. She took a deep breath and squared her shoulders.

"Lieutenant Emma Carpenter," she said. "United States Navy, Intelligence Division, San Diego Station."

Nine

"You're a plant. A navy drone." Rage impaled Seth like a broadsword through the chest. "And you've been *spying* on me?"

Emma's chin fell. "Not exactly. More like... monitoring your activities."

"Sounds a lot like spying."

"Stingray is an important project. We had to be sure the plans didn't fall into the wrong hands."

"And you thought I would sell them to the highest bidder, is that it? Third world countries. Military regimes. Terrorists. Who cares, as long as they can pay cash, right? Is that the kind of person you think I am?"

"No. I mean, at first I wasn't sure. But now—" She shook her head. "Washington is worried about their submarine. Somebody had to play watchdog."

Seth stalked over to Marcus, who looked almost as chagrined as Emma. "You knew about this?"

"Knew about it?" Emma called over his shoulder. "He's the one who picked me for the job."

Marcus nodded haltingly.

Seth's throat constricted until he could hardly force words through it. "And you didn't tell me that naval intelligence had an operative dogging me?"

Marcus kicked the red patio tile miserably. "She's not an operative. She's a junior secretary."

"I was working my way up to operative."

"You picked a secretary to spy on me?"

"Your old secretary had just retired. The navy was getting nervous about all this mess with DeBruzyka and wanted someone to keep an eye on things. I figured if you were looking for a secretary, I'd send you a secretary." Marcus shrugged his broad shoulders. "I didn't mean any harm. Hell, how was I to know you were going to marry her? I mean geez, look at her."

Seth's head snapped up. His fists were in Marcus's shirt before even Marcus could see it coming. "What do you mean, 'look at her'?"

Eyes wide, Marcus held up his hands in surrender. "I just mean, you know, she's not your type."

"Why, because her IQ is bigger than her bust size?"

"No, man. Because she's…nice. Those women you usually go out with have more bite in 'em than a great white."

Seth let go of his cousin's shirt, muttering. "Get in the house. And don't even think about telling anyone else about this."

A full thirty seconds passed in tense silence while Marcus marched. Seth kept a good twenty feet between himself and Emma.

He didn't dare get any closer.

She twisted the engagement ring on her finger. "For what it's worth, I tried to tell you last night."

"It's not worth very damn much."

But even as he said the words, their truth sunk in. She'd broken off a kiss, trying to tell him something, and he hadn't let her.

Because his damned emotions had run away with him. Because he'd found out he was going to have a baby and he'd let himself believe that he could have all the other things he wanted out of life, too. A partner. A wife.

Instead he'd gotten lies.

"You set me up from the beginning. When I was looking for a new assistant, every candidate I interviewed suddenly found a position before I called them back."

She shrugged. "Maybe the navy helped them a little."

"I never wanted to hire you. I wanted someone older. Gray-haired. Coke-bottle glasses. Permanent flotation device around the hips."

"I'm sorry."

She sounded so sincere. Just like a woman.

He dragged a hand through his hair. "You're fired."

"What?"

"You heard me. I'll have your personal effects boxed up and sent to you."

Her chest rose in a stuttering breath, then she nodded sadly. "I suppose I should have expected that."

Her eyes glistened, but her chin never fell, her shoulders never sagged. God, the woman had the heart of a bull whale.

She walked toward him, her hips swaying like the tips of a palm tree in a tropical breeze, but Seth would bet his fortune it wasn't a purposely seductive move. It was part of the innate charm about her. The siren song that called him to forget his past. Throw away his future.

She eased the diamond ring from her finger, gave it one last look, almost as if it meant something to her, and held it out toward him. "I suppose you'll want this back."

The gemstone glittered hypnotically in the starlight. He shook his head as if in a dream.

She put the ring in his palm and closed his fist over it. "I can't keep it, Seth."

Like a striking snake, he grabbed her wrist, held her in place while he slid the white gold band back on her finger.

Understanding rose on a tide of panic in her eyes. "Surely you don't think I'd still marry you."

"I don't think you have a choice."

She tried to pull away, to free her hand, but he held her steady. "I won't do it."

"Why not? I was good enough for Emma Carpenter, pig farmer and secretary. Am I not good enough for Emma Carpenter, naval intelligence officer?"

"That's not the point."

His eyes burned in a pool of hate he'd kept bottled up inside him too long. "Then what is?"

"You—you don't even know me. The real me."

"I know the only thing I need to know about you." He pointed toward her belly button. "That's my baby in there. And I'm not letting you take it away from me. No matter who you are."

"Seth, be reasonable—"

His mouth tasted like sewage. Disease simmered in its depths. "I'm perfectly reasonable. You'll marry me and we'll share this child, or I'll sue for custody and you'll be the one left out in the cold."

"You'd never win."

"My family has a lot of connections in Florida. On top of that, you lied to me about who you were. Got pregnant under false pretenses. I have a stable career, a home. The navy probably moves you around every couple of years. Not to mention the possibility of long sea deployments. I think a judge would take all that into consideration. Are you willing to risk it?''

He saw the second she took him seriously. Her wrist went slack in his grasp. Her lips parted and her breath just…stopped. "My God. You'd do that? You'd take my baby away?"

Guilt shot through him like the shaft from a spear gun, but he didn't let up. Didn't let a single crack show in his facade.

This was a battle he couldn't afford to lose.

"*Our* baby, Emma. A child I have every bit as much right to as you do. Maybe more."

"I told you I wouldn't keep it from you."

"I can't take that chance." He felt his skin, hot against hers. He burned, as if with fever. "I lost one child because I trusted a woman. I won't lose another."

He was holding her so tightly that her hands had gone limp and bloodless white. Her round eyes gleamed wide and frightened in the moonlight.

Afraid.

God, she's afraid of me.

Choking on his own bile, he released her, turned his back on her. But instead of the footsteps scurrying back to the house he expected to hear, he tensed as he heard her step up behind him.

"Is that what Marcus meant about me not knowing what you'd been through? Is it Josh?"

The fire within tempered his body to steel as a festered wound reopened.

"You said you got attached to the boy. Was he your son?"

"No." To his horror, hot tears pumped into his eyes. The rage welled up, unstoppable this time, and spilled out. Onto Emma. "No, but by God, I wish he had been. Maybe then I could have stopped her."

"Who?"

He drew a shaking breath. "Tiffany Seymour. I met her at Harvard. We dated a year or so. Just before I graduated, I broke it off. I was planning to come back to Emerald Cove and she... Well, things weren't working out between us."

Seth sat on a cement bench and buried his face in his hands. "A few months later Tiff showed up here, pregnant."

Emma sat next to him. "What did you do?"

He looked at her sideways. "What do you think?"

"You asked her to marry you?"

He nodded. "But she said she needed time to think about it. Turned out, she needed lots of time. And lots of money. I paid all her medical bills, moved her into my condo, bought her a car. Hell, I bought her anything she wanted. Gave her cash to live off of, set up a trust for the baby. Six months later she had a healthy little boy and for the first time in my life, I fell in love."

"But you said—"

He stood, restlessness getting the better of him, as it always did when he thought back to this time in his life. The moon glittered off the ocean and in the cove, a schooner drifted on a calm sea.

"I tried to love Tiffany, but I didn't. Not really. I only stayed with her because I *did* love being a dad. She left Josh with me a lot while she was out doing God knew what. I liked getting up in the middle of the night to rock him when he cried. I liked the way he smelled after a bath. I liked the feel of him curled up on my chest when we slept. For a year there was nothing I didn't like about him.''

He had to drag the final words out of himself. ''Then one day she told me it had all been a joke. She was taking the baby and heading off to L.A. with another man—a man she'd been seeing since before I'd broken up with her in Massachusetts—and there wasn't a damned thing I could do about it, because *he* was Josh's real father. Not me.''

He heard Emma's sharp intake of shock. ''My God. How cruel.''

He turned to her, eyes burning. ''You aren't the first woman who's ever lied to me, Emma. But by God, you'll be the last. And I *will* have my child. With or without you.''

''Good night, Seth,'' Emma said stiffly, standing in the doorway to her apartment. They were the first words spoken between them in more than half an hour.

He'd driven her home in his fancy BMW. He'd been hard on the clutch and hadn't so much as glanced her way once during the drive. Even now he wouldn't look at her. He stared over her shoulder into her living room. His brown eyes shone like two polished stones. Hard. Glassy.

Inhuman.

It was as if the man she'd known before tonight no longer existed. A replica had been left in his place. One that looked like him, sounded like him, even smelled like him, but that contained none of his true essence. It was as if Seth's spirit, his soul, had been carved out of him, and only emptiness held its place.

When he finally pulled his vacuous gaze down to her, she felt for him. For the pain he'd suffered at having a child he'd loved for nearly a year, a child he believed was his son, ripped from his arms. From his life. She hurt for him as only another parent could. She'd only carried the tiny being inside her for a couple of weeks, and already she couldn't imagine life without it.

She ached for Seth's loss, but that didn't mean she accepted what he was doing to her now because of it.

She tried to close the door, but his immovable frame blocked the way. "You can't think I'm going to invite you in."

Not after he'd threatened to take her baby away.

Not after the way he'd kissed her the last time he'd stood in her living room.

The flowers he'd sent still stood in a vase on the dining table. She'd throw them out later.

He shook his head slowly. "We're going to have to do something with your furniture," he said hollowly.

"*Do* something?"

"We could sell it, I suppose. But it might be better to donate it to charity."

"Give it away? You want to give away my furniture?" Her fists instinctively clenched on her hips. Her voice rose an octave.

"The condo's going to be a bit crowded, otherwise. Of course, if there are a few pieces you want to keep—"

"How gracious of you, letting me keep my own furniture!"

He finally looked at her again, his eyes cold and passionless, as if he couldn't imagine why she was upset. "I'm just trying to be practical."

She folded her arms over her chest, hands molded into fists. The posture helped temper her urge to hit him—if only to try to knock some reaction out of him. Anything other than this deadpan monotone.

"Who said I'm moving into your condo?"

Finally, some expression. Even if it was only one cocked eyebrow. "Surely you didn't think we'd get married and live separately."

"Surely not," she mocked, and stalked into the living room, leaving the door open behind her.

"I thought you weren't inviting me in."

"I didn't." She could tell from the direction of his voice that he'd followed her inside.

"You left the door open."

She wheeled and found him right behind her. They stood nose to chest. "Should I have slammed it in your face? Would you have gotten the message then that I don't want you in my life? That the only reason I'm even speaking to you is because you threatened me?"

"I told you, I have no choice." Did his voice sound a bit rougher? Maybe she was getting through to him.

"There's always a choice, Seth. What you're doing to me is as bad as what that woman, Tiffany, did to you. You're using my baby to hold me hostage."

"You're no hostage. You can walk away anytime you want. All you have to do is sign over your parental rights."

Of course. She tried not to let him get to her, but her eyes stung. Of course she wasn't the one he wanted. "And leave my baby behind."

"You said you didn't want to get pregnant."

"I said I wouldn't have chosen to get pregnant. That doesn't mean I'd turn my back on my baby. Or that I don't love it more than anything else in life."

"Then we're right back where we started. Getting married."

She swallowed hard. There had to be an alternative.

Not exactly where they started, she thought. There would be no more passionate embraces between them. No heated kisses. Just cold, lifeless hate.

He advanced until he towered over her once again. "Despite what you think, I'm not like Tiffany. I won't take the baby from you unless you force my hand." He put his hands on her shoulders. She'd been wrong about him being cold and lifeless. Heat radiated from his fingers, anger poured off him, searing her bare skin. "But I won't let you take my son or daughter from me, either."

A vivid memory of him holding her differently, tenderly, burst through her mind. The burning on her shoulders became unbearable. She jerked away. "Don't touch me."

"Don't worry. I don't plan to."

She rubbed her hands over the imprints his fingers had left and looked up at him uncertainly.

His eyes narrowed. "I'll force you into my home if I have to. But I won't force you into my bed."

"Of course not," she chided. "Wouldn't want to make that mistake again, would you?"

He watched her silently a second, and it seemed that something in him softened, though she couldn't be sure through her tear-clouded eyes.

"If I made a mistake in sleeping with you," he said quietly, "it was only in doing it when I didn't have any way to protect you. And for that, I am truly sorry."

The tears in her eyes now clogged her throat, as well. "Not sorry enough to walk away."

"No. Not that sorry."

She sank onto her couch and rested her hand over

the abdomen that would soon swell. "So we're going to get married, live together, raise a child together and...never touch each other. Never laugh, or tease, or get jealous, or argue, or love."

"I wouldn't count on the never arguing part."

"That's not funny. What kind of life will our child have without love?"

"Our baby will have plenty of love. I'll love it. You'll love it. We just won't love each other. A lot of kids grow up with worse." He drew a slow breath and let it out even more slowly, then sat next to her, being careful not to touch her. "For the baby and our families, we can make our marriage look as real as possible. As for what happens between us in private, that's our business."

Despite Seth's assurances, she knew exactly what kind of life she would have with Seth: lackluster, lonely, full of endless, repetitive days.

She'd be a burden, a stone around his neck, and eventually he would come to hate her even more than he already did.

Seemingly oblivious to her distress, he leaned back and propped one ankle on the opposite knee. "Pack a bag, Emma. I want you at my condo. Tonight."

Ten

Cinderemma lifted a breakfast plate from the soapy water, rinsed it and set it in the dishwasher to dry. The hem of her patchwork skirt swished above her bare feet, and her threadbare blouse clung to her chest.

Outside the window, a pair of starlings bobbed on the breeze, their wings a blur of motion.

"Cinderemma," they sang, "oh, Cinderemma. It's a beautiful day. Can you come out and play?"

Despite her unhappiness, Cinderemma smiled. "Alas, I cannot, I have too much work today."

"Cinderemma has work," one nightingale chirped, wings fluttering.

"Work, work, work," the second bird chirped back. "Cinderemma always has work."

The birds dipped and dove in circles, as if chasing each other. "Her wicked stepmother won't let her come out and play."

Cinderemma laughed at her little friends' antics. "Not my stepmother, but the one who locks me away is definitely wicked." She waved the birds away. "Now go on. Go and play without me to—"

"Emma?" The bass voice behind her would never be mistaken for a bird.

Emma turned, feeling a flush creep up her neck.

Seth glanced around the room. "Did you say something?"

"Me? No."

She set the plate she was holding in the dishwasher before she dropped it. Bad enough that her mind wandered off like that, but to be caught at it. Again...

Seth leaned one shoulder against the refrigerator and folded his arms over his chest. "You could have let the machine do the washing. That's what it's for."

She could have, but it seemed a waste of energy for just two place settings. Besides, she'd been daydreaming, and it had been a suffersome one. What kind of story would it have been if the wicked stepmother had given Cinderella a three-cycle Kenmore to scrub her pots and pans?

Who said she had to scrub his pots and pans, anyway?

Emma dried her hands on the towel beside the sink and looked down her nose at Seth. "Better yet, I could have let you wash your own damned dishes."

She started to jaunt out of the kitchen, but before she reached the door, his big body was in front of her. The fresh scent of him, up close, made her wobble for a moment, as if she'd stepped from terra firma onto the deck of a boat. It took her a moment to find her sea legs.

"So why didn't you make me wash my own damned dishes?"

"Maybe I was grateful for the distraction. Something to do. Anything besides sit in this condo and stare at the walls." She dipped around him and headed for the dining room.

He followed.

"Don't you have anywhere to go?" she asked.

"Anything to do? I thought you had a company to run."

"I am running it." As if to prove it, he sat in front of the laptop on the dining room table and calmly tapped in a few commands. The computer beeped obligingly.

"Oh, really? I would have thought you were too busy watching every move I make."

"I haven't been watching you," he said placidly.

She threw her hands up. "Seth, it would be hard for you not to. We haven't been out of this house in three days!"

"We can go out. Where do you want me to take you?"

"I don't want you to *take* me anywhere. I want some personal time. I want to be alone. I want to be *free*."

He tapped on the computer keyboard. "Not an option."

One stride carried her to his side. With her palm, she slapped the lid to the laptop closed, nearly catching his fingers. "You can't keep me a prisoner here."

Finally, he looked up at her. "You're not a prisoner."

"Am I missing something?" she said, her voice sounding more desperate than she would have liked. "You won't let me leave."

"You can go anywhere you want. As long as I'm with you."

"Ugh! How long do you think you can watch me night and day?"

"As long as it takes."

"Until after the baby is born," she guessed.

He didn't bother to acknowledge. They both knew

he didn't have to. She turned her back on him and paced across the thick cream carpet. When she came back, she planted herself in front of him, hands braced on the table, her nose to his. "You may see me as a doltish office drone, but—"

She stumbled over her words. His gaze had dropped beneath her eyes. Beneath her chin. Lower. Too late, she realized by leaning over him, she'd offered him a view straight down the open collar of her blouse.

Slowly he dragged his gaze up again. "If that's how I saw you, we wouldn't be in this situation, would we?"

Refusing to give in to the urge to straighten up, to button her collar all the way to her chin, she met his hard eyes squarely. "I am a highly trained member of the United States Navy," she said through her teeth. "If I really wanted to get away, I'd already be gone."

"Then why aren't you?" he asked softly.

The question splashed over her like a surprise hit from a water balloon. She could have left anytime. He might have followed her, but he wouldn't have stopped her. Not if it had come down to a physical confrontation. Seth stirred a lot of uncomfortable feelings in her mind and in her blood when she was close to him, but worry for her safety wasn't one of them.

"Maybe because I'm trying to work things out between us like an adult. Maybe because I need to prove to you—to both of us—that I'm not like the woman who hurt you."

Drawing on a daring she didn't know she possessed, she reached out and feathered her fingers over the furrows in his brow. "Maybe because beneath all that anger you're blowing my way, I see the fear in your eyes."

He jerked his head back, shoved his chair out and stood. Without a glance at her, he walked to the window and stared out at the cove. She waited in silence while he struggled with his demons.

"You're telling me that you'll stay?" he finally asked, his voice husky. "That you want to stay?"

She wouldn't lie to him. He'd been lied to too much already. "To be honest, I'm not sure what I want. But when I figure it out, you'll be the first one to know. I promise you that much."

"It's not just that I'm afraid you'll take off on me." He pulled in a deep breath and let it out slowly. "Someone tried to kill me with the bomb on the catamaran. Now that we're...connected, you could be a target, too."

"They'd have nothing to gain from hurting me. I don't even work for you anymore, remember?" She walked slowly toward him. With each step nearer she got, his eyes dilated, darkened.

"I remember."

She stopped in front of him and looked up at him. "Even if they did try something, I can take care of myself. And hiding out here isn't going to help us figure out who planted the explosives, or why."

"*We* are not going to figure out anything. *You* are going to leave Stingray and its security to me."

"But I could help. I—"

"I know. You're a highly trained member of the United States Navy." Every muscle in his body tensed. "You're also pregnant. No way you're going anywhere near Evans Yachts or Stingray until this is over."

She opened her mouth to argue, then realized he

was right. She had a baby to think about, even if she didn't believe she was in any danger.

"Okay," she admitted, then looked up at him despondently. "But I can't just sit here, and neither can you. I've got to do something. I've got to get out. And you've got a submarine to build."

He dragged a hand across the back of his neck, massaging his muscles. "You want to do something, go visit with my mother. She's dying to talk about wedding plans, and Marcus has plenty of security posted around the estate. You'll be safe there."

"Where will you be?"

"Working. I have a submarine to build, remember? And don't bother to argue. This is the best offer you're going to get."

She chewed on her lip a moment, then said, "I'll take it."

Any offer was progress, as far as she was concerned.

She hurried into the guest bedroom to brush her hair. A moment later she was back with her purse in one hand and a pair of sandals in the other, nearly giddy with excitement.

For the first time in days, she was going to be free.

Even though the breakfast hour was long gone, the kitchen in Gideon Faulkner's seaside bungalow smelled like maple syrup. Seth ran his palm across the scarred butcher-block table in the cozy room with buttery yellow walls and matching gingham curtains. Sunlight lanced through the window over the sink and cut a golden swath to the Mason jar of silk sunflowers adorning the center of the table.

As bright and welcoming as the room was, the

warmest glow didn't come from the Florida sunshine or any of the homey furnishings. That effect belonged to Gideon's wife, Brooke.

Gideon's gaze followed her every move as she refilled first Seth's tumbler, and then his own, from a pitcher of fresh lemonade. She smiled shyly at her husband as she poured, and Seth watched them curiously—the way her fingertips brushed his arm as she leaned over him, the way his hand rested on the gentle swell of her abdomen where their baby grew. The connection between husband and wife pulsed and breathed with every glance between them, every touch.

Feeling like a voyeur even though there was nothing overtly intimate in the newlyweds' actions, Seth shifted uncomfortably in his chair. He couldn't help but compare Gideon and Brooke's affection for each other with the harsh anxiety that laced his relationship with Emma. And he couldn't help but feel sorry that he and Emma would never know the kind of bond that warmed this house.

With her hand on Gideon's shoulder, Brooke gestured toward the window, and the two men in hard hats pretending to trim trees back from the power line beyond it. "You think I should offer some lemonade to our navy watchdogs outside?"

Gideon took her free hand in his. "As much as I'm sure they'd appreciate the cold drink, I think they'd prefer not to jeopardize their cover." He patted her playfully on the backside. "And Marcus would have a cow if he caught you coddling his men."

"Hey." She stepped out of his reach. "Watch it, buster, or I won't be coddling you tonight, either."

Gideon held up his hands in mock surrender.

Brooke winked at Seth. "How about you? Can I get you something else? I've got some pita bread and some smoked turkey. I could make sandwiches."

"None for me, thanks." He couldn't stay. He couldn't explain why, exactly, but he felt...restless. Anxious to catch up to Emma, both because he wasn't as sure as she was that whoever had sabotaged the catamaran would have no interest in her, and because he couldn't quash the unreasonable fear that she'd left town.

He wanted to believe her when she said she wouldn't run off, but trusting a woman—especially a woman carrying his child—just didn't come easy to him.

Gideon declined lunch as well, though his gaze lingered on the empty doorway long seconds after Brooke had left.

Seth frowned. "You okay?"

"Yeah, sure. Why wouldn't I be?"

"You looked a little lost there, for a minute." Seth glanced at the workmen outside. "From what you've told me, you spent most of your life sequestered away, buried in work. Watched over." He glanced toward the men pruning trees outside. "Just thought maybe you and Brooke needed some time for yourselves, especially with the baby coming. Time to live a little."

Gideon hunched over a beat-up laptop that appeared to be held together by spliced wires and duct tape. "I appreciate your concern. But I don't mind hard work as long as it's my choice, not someone else's command. And Brooke and I are managing to squeeze in a little living between all the slave driving." His fingers paused over his keyboard. "Last night she introduced me to the fine sport of skinny-dipping."

Seth winced. Involuntarily, he glanced outside again. "I wouldn't have thought that was much of a spectator sport."

A hint of color tinged Gideon's cheeks. "Ah, we ditched them first."

"You hope." He knew firsthand how deceptive those intelligence types could be.

Gideon tipped his chair onto the two back legs and laughed. "Well, if we didn't, they got quite a show." Setting his chair right, he looked down the hall where Brooke had disappeared. "She's great, isn't she?"

Seth studied his juice glass. "Is this one of those trick questions where, if I answer yes, you get mad because you're jealous and if I answer no, you get mad because you're offended?"

"No."

"Then yes. She's great. And you, my friend, are totally smitten."

"It's that obvious?"

"Oh, yeah."

Gideon pecked a few more keys then stopped again, grinning that silly, terrified, grin Seth had seen on countless men about to become fathers for the first time. "Man, getting married, having a baby, building a great sub pretty much all at once. It's amazing, isn't it?"

"Yeah. Great." Seth tried to put up a good front, saw in Gideon's expression that he failed.

"So why don't you look happy?"

"It's…complicated."

Gideon stopped typing and looked toward the doorway where his wife had disappeared. As if he could still see her there, his eyelids fell half-closed. His voice grew husky. "Not if you love her, it's not. It's the simplest thing on earth."

The sentiment rumbled through Seth's stomach like a bowling ball. He felt something for Emma. He just didn't know what. The truth was, he wasn't sure he would recognize love if it stood up and bit him in the ass. He hadn't allowed himself to feel it in too long.

Then there was the fact that he was blackmailing her into marrying him. Which brought him right back to complicated.

But Gideon didn't need to know that. Luckily, the trill of Seth's cell phone prevented him from having to explain.

"I'm sorry," Holt complained breathlessly. "They had me outnumbered and outgunned. I couldn't stop them."

Seth's grip tightened on the phone. "Stop who? What the hell are you talking about?"

"Mom, Laura and Emma. They're gone."

Delray's Restaurant and Seafood Grill sat on a gentle rise that couldn't quite be called a hill above Emerald Cove's busiest marina. This morning three women sat among the polished silver and linen-covered tables for a champagne brunch just this side of heaven.

"Free at last! Free at last! Thank the Lord, I'm free at last!" Laura Evans hooted. Seth's sister looked like she'd come straight from a dive. Her hair was swept back in a short ponytail and Emma could just make out the neckline of a swimsuit under her Marine Institute T-shirt.

"Martin Luther King?" Emma asked, unfolding a napkin onto her lap.

Laura nodded. "And Laura Evans, upon her escape from the Evans State Penitentiary."

Lynn Evans, elegant as ever in a sleek violet silk blouse and tailored slacks, tssked her daughter. "Your father and brother are just being attentive, dear."

Laura snorted. "Last night Holt chased me halfway down the driveway just to offer to carry the garbage out to the front gate for me."

"He was being helpful. What's wrong with that?"

"Mom," Laura said dryly. "He'd been about to take a shower. He wasn't wearing anything but a towel. Something is going on."

Emma glanced nervously from Lynn to Laura Evans. She was going to have to talk with Seth about clueing his whole family into what was going on.

But for now she'd settle for a pleasant meal without a big, brooding male hanging over her shoulder. She cleared her throat. "Seth tells me that espionage isn't unusual in yacht racing. They're probably just worried someone is going to steal the secrets to Holt's new boat."

Laura picked up her fork and stabbed a piece of tuna steak. "Yeah, I'll admit it is kind of freaky. The fire on Seth's boat and the break-in at the office, all in the same weekend." Her face pinched. "You don't suppose they know more than they're telling us?"

Mrs. Evans gave her daughter an endearing look. "Darling, men always know more than they tell us. The trick to finding out how much more is to go along as if you don't have a clue. If you confront them, they clam up. If you play along, they always spill it. Eventually."

Laura sipped her orange juice, considering. Emma waved the waiter over to refill her coffee. She didn't

like the direction of this conversation. A change o
subject was definitely in order. But to what? She'
never had many girlfriends and didn't have a clue wha
women talked about over brunch.

She improvised. "Laura, how is your work at th
marina going?"

Laura's face brightened. "Fantastic. We're makin
real progress."

"That's wonderful, dear."

"Thanks, Mom. And thanks for asking, Emma. I
case you haven't noticed, the manly contingent of th
Evans family isn't too thrilled with my work with th
reefs."

"Your father and your brothers love you, honey.'

"They want me to build boats," Laura said flatly
She turned to Emma. "I just couldn't stand to be a
office drone, you know?"

"Yeah, I do."

Laura's eyes rounded. "No offense intended."

"None taken."

Emma's cell phone chimed out the tones of "Th
Star-Spangled Banner," saving them all from wha
could have been an awkward moment. Emma excuse
herself from the table and stepped onto the balcon
over the water to take the call.

"Where the hell are you?" The snarl beneath Seth'
words might have irritated Emma, but she heard th
concern beneath the anger. For reasons that escape
her, his worry set off a sympathetic vibration dee
inside her.

"Delray's," she said in as cheerful a tone as sh
could muster. "Where are you?"

She heard tires squeal as if he'd made a sudde
U-turn.

"On my way." Each word clanged a warning.

"I'll let Laura and your mother know you'll be joining us," she said.

He must have heard a bit of warning in her overly sweet voice. For a moment, she only heard his harsh breathing, then he said, almost contritely, "Damn it, Emma, you were supposed to stay with Holt."

"Unfortunately your mother and sister didn't know that."

"You're telling me this was their idea?"

"The way your father and Holt have been hovering, they're feeling as cloistered as I am. Only they have no idea why they're under house arrest. Would you rather I'd have let them make their great escape on their own? At least I know to keep my guard up."

A moment of silence passed. "I thought you didn't think there was any danger to anyone not directly connected to the project."

"I don't. But that doesn't mean I believe in tempting fate. Seth, you've got to tell them what's going on, for their own good."

"The fewer people know about...the other project, the better."

"Is that it? Or are you holding back because you don't want to worry the womenfolk's pretty little empty heads with details like the truth?" Her voice dripped southern sweetness.

"All right, you made your point. I'll talk to Pop and Holt. Now just stay put and keep your eyes open. I'll be there in five."

The connection went dead before she even had a chance to say goodbye. Drawing a deep, calming breath, she returned to the table.

"Everything all right, dear? You look a little pale," Mrs. Evans said as Emma sat.

"I'm fine. But that was Seth on the phone." She stabbed a forkful of cold swordfish steak and threw the two Evans women an apologetic smile. "I'm afraid the bloodhounds have picked up our trail."

His pulse hammering, Seth brought his Z3 to a lurching stop in Delray's parking lot. A quick scan of the area reassured him that nothing was amiss, but his heartbeat refused to settle. A sense of urgency he couldn't explain drove him out of his car and toward the restaurant, toward Emma, in a hurried step. He was ten feet away before he realized his briefcase—with his eight-thousand-dollar laptop inside—lay on the passenger seat of the convertible, easy pickings for any thief. He almost kept walking anyway. Almost.

The sight of Emma waving at him over the railing on Delray's front porch changed his mind. She looked fine. Better than fine. As mouthwateringly delectable as any dish served in the restaurant behind her.

She'd been waiting for him. It wouldn't do to have her see him like this—palms sweaty, breathing rapid and shallow, stumbling over his own feet in his rush to get to her. Geez, she'd probably think he was some kind of obsessive lunatic.

Clenching his fists with the effort not to run to her, he stopped, turned slowly and headed back to his car. Out of his peripheral vision he saw her frown and start down the steps toward him.

He kept walking.

Leaning into his car to retrieve the briefcase, he risked another glance her way. Casually. As if he wasn't in the middle of a full-blown panic attack for which he had no explanation. Blood pounded in his ears, but he straightened slowly, tried to smile and acknowledged her wave with a nod of his head.

Behind her, a dark SUV rolled slowly through the parking lot toward the stairway she descended. Through the deeply tinted windows, Seth could just make out the form of a driver, a man, and maybe a passenger. The hairs stood on the back of his sweat-dampened neck.

He had been planning on putting the briefcase in the trunk. The hell with it. He didn't want to waste the time. Hand fisted tightly around the leather handle, he started toward Emma.

The SUV was about twenty-five feet behind her, still cruising slowly forward.

Seth walked more quickly, devouring the asphalt surface between them in long strides. He made it halfway across the lot and was starting to relax, thinking he was being paranoid, when the SUV's engine roared to life. Tires squealed, spun, then caught traction. The vehicle leaped forward like a gigantic cat.

He knew the second Emma recognized the danger. Her face froze. She stumbled, looking over her shoulder.

A thunderous rage crashing through his mind, Seth ran toward her from her front while the dark truck closed in on her from behind. He was almost there. Twenty feet. Fifteen.

But the SUV was faster. He wasn't going to make it.

He shouted at her and waved. "Jump! Jump!"

He had no idea if she heard him, but with the SUV's bumper on her heels, she dove between two parked cars. Seth kept running, sure the truck would stop, the driver drag her inside. Take her away from him.

He tried to see her but the SUV was between him and her hiding spot. Only then did he realize the SUV had passed Emma by without notice. It was gaining speed. Still coming.

At him.

Briefly he felt the heat of an engine, smelled oil before he heard the sickening thud of flesh on metal. The impact tossed him onto the hood like a bullfighter onto the horns of his two-thousand-pound Brahma. The sun whirled over his head. The breath whooshed out of him. Blinding white pain shot through his hip, ribs and shoulder like a string of popping firecrackers when he connected with the windshield.

Then there was nothing but air beneath him. He saw the palm trees lining the boulevard behind him. The bobbing masts of the boats at dock. He felt the breeze rustle his hair. He was floating. Down. Down. The ground rushing up to greet him.

He hit hard. Blackness exploded around him, inside him, and as if someone had flicked off a switch, his world went dark.

Eleven

The sound of brisk footsteps echoing down the hall toward the waiting room of the Emerald Cove Medical Center brought Emma to her feet. For a moment she thought the crisp stride belonged to—

No, it couldn't be. A quick glance down toward the door confirmed she'd only been thinking wishfully. Seth and his brother had similar mannerisms, that was all. A comparable gait when they were worried.

Laura launched herself at the younger of the Evans brothers, stopping him in the waiting room door. She buried her face in his shoulder. "Oh, God. I'm so glad you're here."

Holt wrapped his arms around his sister, but his blue eyes, haggard and afraid, met Emma's over Laura's shoulder. "How is he?"

"Stable is all they'll tell us." Emma's lower lip trembled so hard she had to bite it to keep it still. "The doctors are still working on him."

He turned his gaze to his mother, who sat pale and brittle on a lumpy orange couch. Dragging his sister with him, Holt went to her, sat between them and managed to get an arm around each.

"Where's Dad?" he asked.

Lynn Evans's eyes glistened. "He had a golf game this morning. He must have his cell phone turned off.

But the club sent someone out to look for him. And
Marcus is on his way, too.''

Giving them one good squeeze, Holt left his mother
and sister on the couch and paced the length the room.
It was clear from the look on his face that Emma was
the one he wanted to talk to.

He tugged her into the hall by her elbow and
dragged a hand over his head, setting his blond hair
on end. ''What the hell happened?''

''A car—an SUV, black, I think. It—it went right
for him. It hit him on purpose.''

Blue flames lit his eyes. ''Did you get a license
plate?''

''No. I'm sorry, but it was behind me. And then—''
She choked, fought to swallow the hard lump in her
throat. ''Then Seth…''

''Any chance Mom or Laura could ID the vehicle?''

''No. They were still in the restaurant.'' Thank
heavens for that. Bad enough she would have night-
mares. No need for all of them to suffer. ''There
weren't any other witnesses.''

Holt's shoulders slumped. He wrapped an arm
around her shaking shoulders. ''It's all right.'' He
scanned the empty hallway. ''Damn it, where is everybody? Why don't they tell us something?''

As if on command, a large-boned African-American
nurse wearing neon orange scrubs pushed through a
pair of double doors across the hall. ''Ms. Carpenter?''
she called nasally, eyes searching the knot of people
in the waiting room.

Emma ducked from beneath Holt's arm. ''I'm
Emma Carpenter.''

''Follow me.'' The nurse didn't wait for acknowledgment, just led Emma into a large round room

with six curtained areas set around it, like the spokes of a wheel.

In one, Seth struggled with two wiry orderlies while a nurse loomed over him with a syringe. ''No.'' He grabbed the nurse's arm, held her away. The orderlies tried to push him down, but he managed to lever himself halfway up anyway, grimacing in pain. The sheet that had been pulled up over his bare chest slipped down far enough for Emma to see that his upper torso wasn't the only part of him that was bare. The flesh of his hip looked painfully bruised and swollen.

''Not until I see Emma,'' he growled, still struggling with the emergency room staff. He gained enough freedom to throw his head back and howl. ''Emma!''

She was at his side before she realized she'd moved. She brushed her hand over his brow. ''Hey, easy there, big guy.''

He turned to her, his brown eyes clouded by shock and pain. He reached up, but the IV tube stopped him short of touching her. ''Emma,'' he said more quietly, as if not quite sure he believed she was there.

''I'm here.''

The nurse took advantage of his momentary distraction to shove the needle into the IV tubing and depress the plunger. ''That should settle him.'' Then she and the orderlies left.

Emma turned her attention back to Seth. Now that he lay still, she could see the white creases that pain fanned out from the corners of his mouth and eyes. Gently she eased the sheet back to his chest.

''You're here,'' he said.

''Did you think I wouldn't come?''

''I was afraid.''

A knot of frustration hardened in her chest. "Still think I'm going to ditch you the first chance I get? Even if it means leaving you lying unconscious in a parking lot?"

He turned his head away from her. His jaw set, and she didn't think it was from the pain. "Just after I got hit—before I even hit the ground—I could have sworn I saw the SUV stop. I was afraid they were turning around to come back for a second pass. At you. I was afraid for you."

The knot in her chest unraveled like a cheap sweater. Her eyes drifted closed. When she opened them, she turned his head back toward her with a finger on his chin, careful not to touch the raw scrape on his cheek.

"I'm sorry," she said, hoping he knew she meant it. Not sure what else to say, she confirmed what he'd seen. "The van did come back, but not to hit me. One of the men got out and picked up your briefcase."

Seth's face twisted in what looked like a combination of pain and frustration. "My laptop. That's what they were after all along."

"Your computer?"

"It was in my briefcase. I'd been working at Gideon's. They must have thought—"

"Stingray."

He nodded. "Then the project's been compromised." Her chest hurt, knowing what it would mean to Seth to lose the plans to his sub. What it would mean to America. "I told the police about the theft already, but they didn't seem optimistic about getting your briefcase back. We have to call the admiral."

"No. There was nothing on my hard drive they can use. I wouldn't risk the project like that."

She drew a rattled breath. ''Okay, then. That's good. They've got one useless laptop and you appear to be more or less in one piece, so how about we start this over. Pretend I just walked in.''

Staring at her darkly, he didn't look like a man who wanted to play make-believe.

''So,'' she said. ''Are you in one piece?'' She resisted the urge to touch his bruised chest. To feel for herself that the heart underneath was still whole.

''Would it matter to you if I wasn't?'' There was a rough edge on his voice.

She paused, not sure how to answer. Of course it would matter to her, though she wasn't sure he'd believe it. This was a man she'd worked with. Survived a disaster with. Made love with in a thatch hut with a tropical storm providing the mood music. Whatever had happened between them since, those things couldn't be erased.

''I don't want to see you hurt,'' she finally said.

His hand snaked out from beneath the cover and clasped hers. Was that relief that softened the pain lines at the corners of his mouth?

''Then yes,'' he said, his voice raw, whether with pain or emotion she couldn't say. ''I'm okay.''

She stacked her other hand on their joined hands, emotion rising suddenly within her as the memory of him sailing head over heels through the air assailed her. She squeezed her eyes shut, but the vision wouldn't go away. ''God, Seth. I've never seen anything like what happened to you.'' She opened her eyes, looked at him through a veil of tears. ''I thought you were dead.''

''That makes two of us. But Nurse Ratchet that just left assures me this isn't hell, despite her resemblance to a certain fallen angel. And I hurt too much to be in heaven, so I must be alive still.''

Emma chuckled and wiped her nose with a corner of his sheet. ''How can you joke? That SUV hit you head-on, and you didn't even try to get out of the way.''

''I know. Stupid. But I saw it coming up behind you, and all I could think about was getting to you first.''

Her insides softened like chocolate left out in the sun. ''You were trying to save me?''

He opened the fingers of the hand she held and brushed them over her blouse where it covered her navel. ''Both of you,'' he said.

Of course. He would do anything to protect his baby. Silly of Emma to think she entered the equation as anything other than the vessel that carried his unborn child.

Or so she thought until he stretched his fingers an inch farther, caught her shirt between them and tugged her toward him. When he had her close enough, he let go of her blouse and reached up to cup her cheek.

''I thought I was going to lose you, Emma.''

Her. Not just the baby.

''Lose you before I had a chance to tell—''

His eyelids fluttered. From the way he slurred his words, Emma guessed whatever the nurse had given him was finally taking hold.

''A chance to tell me what, Seth?''

''Tell you…'' He swallowed, struggled visibly to focus. ''I saw Gideon and Brooke. Watched 'em. Made me want to tell you…''

He struggled again for lucidity. Struggled and lost.

His eyelids settled closed, and Emma doubted they'd open again anytime soon.

"Tell you...I..." he whispered, then licked his lips. "I...want to...hmummph. "

"Hmummph?" She shook him gently. "Seth? What does that mean."

She couldn't be right, of course, but she almost thought it sounded like, "I love you."

Probably just the drugs talking.

Leaning heavily on the hall wall, Seth limped toward the living room. Halfway to his destination, he had to stop and rest. His muscles were screaming, his ribs ached. After a day in the hospital and two in bed at home, he still felt like he had glass shards in every joint and barbed wire twined around every muscle. It hurt to move.

It hurt to think about moving.

But even with two cracked ribs, a strained knee, a separated shoulder and a goose egg on the back of his head, lying in bed—alone—was worse. Especially knowing that if he didn't get up and about on his own, Emma would soon come after him, torturing him with her coolly efficient ministrations and concerned eyes.

He had no idea why she'd been so good to him the past few days, after the way he'd treated her. He just knew he couldn't take her undeserved compassion anymore. Not without sacrificing the few shreds of self-respect he had left.

Dredging up the willpower to take two more steps, he made it to the living room and leaned against the entrance to catch his breath. The sliding glass doors to the patio were open, letting in another perfect south Florida day. Stevie Nicks's "Trouble in Shangri-La" played softly on the radio and the room smelled like warm wheat bread.

Emma sat on the sofa, two pieces of buttered brown toast on the coffee table in front of her. She had on a pair of those pants hemmed just below the knee, leaving her slim calves exposed. Her bare feet were tucked up beneath her on the cushion as she flipped through the pages of a glossy women's magazine.

The scene was so intensely peaceful, so pleasant, that it almost felt surreal, given the state of chaos his life was in.

An image of her a year from now, in the same pose, but with a sleeping baby curled in the crook of one arm, punched him as solidly as a fist in the gut. In his mind's eye the infant's pudgy legs shifted silently. A tiny fist kneaded his mother's breast, his life-sustaining instinct to suckle, to nurse, strong even in sleep.

Seth would have been content just to stand and daydream, unnoticed, all morning, but Emma looked up, her green eyes as dazzling as the day outside. "Seth, you're up. What's wrong? Do you need something?"

A fist of hard emotion hit him right in the gut. A whole host of emotions he didn't know how to handle roiled inside him.

God, she was gorgeous when she looked at him like that. So honest. So sincere. As if he was something more to her than the bastard who got her pregnant and then blackmailed her into agreeing to marry him by threatening to keep her child from her. He'd trapped her in a relationship she didn't want, forced her from her home, and now because of him, she couldn't even walk the streets safely.

He didn't deserve her sincerity.

Didn't deserve her.

"What I need is to stretch my legs," he roughed out around the guilt clogging his throat. Pulling his back up as straight as he could, he let go of the wall and stepped into the living room, hoping to hell he didn't fall on his face before he made it to a chair.

She watched him through narrowed eyes, but made no move to help him. Thank God. There were limits to what a man's ego could take, and he was close to his.

He fell into the chair with a painful *oomph,* breathing ridiculously hard considering he hadn't walked twenty feet.

Emma winced. "Okay?"

When he could breath normally again, he nodded. "Marcus should be here any minute."

"Your doctor's appointment. It was nice of him to offer to drive you. I'll feel better knowing there's a SEAL watching out for you."

"You could have a former SEAL watching out for you, too. It's not too late for me to ask Drew to stay with you."

She shook her head. "I don't need a baby-sitter."

"Yeah, I figured you'd say that." He reached to the back of his waistband and pulled out the 9 millimeter Walther PPK he'd tucked there. "Which is why I want you to keep this."

She frowned, not taking the gun he held out to her. "Where did that come from?"

"My sock drawer."

"I meant how long have you had it."

He checked the slide and chambered a round. "Since I graduated from Boy Scouts and learned that

'Be Prepared' has a whole different connotation in the real world. How come you look so surprised?''

''You just don't seem the type to use a gun. I thought you preferred negotiation.''

He took her hand and wrapped it around the butt of the pistol. ''Every good negotiator has an ace in the hole. I assume you know how to use one of these.''

''I'm a good shot.''

One corner of his mouth crooked up. ''Somehow I knew you would be.''

Her face remained impassive, but her eyes smiled back at him. Her silent laughter coiled inside him, soothing the bruises, easing the aching muscles and then starting an ache of a whole new kind.

Seth pushed her wavy hair behind her ear, awed at the way her cheeks flushed pink when he touched her. Wondering how her color would change if he did more than brush his hand across her cheek, then realizing he didn't have to wonder.

He remembered. Remembered her skin, hot and flushed deep burgundy, next to his.

A wave of heat crashed over him. His pulse grew heavy, his breath deep. He brushed his thumb across her parted lips and leaned toward her, hardly noticing the pain in his ribs.

Luckily, the doorbell rang, stopping him from doing anything really stupid.

Like kissing her.

She jerked back as if woken from a dream.

He stood, gritting his teeth at the knife's blade of pain the movement slashed across his ribs. Before he'd even cleared the white spots from his vision, Emma had tucked the pistol under a cushion and opened the door.

Marcus and Emma exchanged a quick embrace, and Seth's jaw hardened despite himself. He should be glad they were getting along better. He had no reason to be jealous of a brief familial hug, and yet, unreasonably, it bothered him to see her touching any other man. Even his stalwart cousin.

"All right," he said, breaking them up. "Let's get a move on. We're going to be late."

They turned to him, Marcus stone-faced and Emma looking inquisitive. No doubt she'd heard the resentful undertones in his voice.

Well, there was nothing he could do about it now, in front of Marcus. He'd just have to apologize for it later. There were a lot of things he needed to apologize for, if he could just find the right time, the right place.

The courage.

"You sure you're ready?" Marcus drawled.

"Yeah," Seth answered. "We're outta here."

An uncharacteristic smile lit Marcus's face as he looked Seth up and down. "Uh, you might want to rethink that plan a minute."

Seth looked down at himself and swore softly. He'd managed to wriggle a pair of jeans over his gray knit boxers when he'd climbed out of bed, but socks had seemed beyond his physical abilities, as had lifting his arms to get a shirt over his head. And the minuscule modesty to be gained by fastening his fly hadn't seemed worth the effort of cramming five brass buttons through the stiff denim one-handed.

"Come on, big guy." Saving him the embarrassment of having to admit in front of his superhuman cousin that he couldn't dress himself, Emma led him toward the bedroom. "Let's get you decent."

* * *

Emma dug around Seth's closet until she found a pair of loafers he could wear without socks, then fished for a button-front shirt. He looked one hundred percent better today.

She was glad to see him recovering. But in a way it made her sad. More correctly, it made her anxious. While he'd been incapacitated, there'd been an unspoken truce between them. She'd fed him, cleaned him, fetched him his medicine every six hours to the second. Some might call her foolish for taking care of a man who had threatened and blackmailed her. Maybe it was. She didn't care.

He'd been vulnerable. He needed her, and being needed pushed away the painful memories of being nothing but a burden as a child. The fears that she would spend the next eighteen years of her life as Seth's burden. Taking care of him gave her a taste of independence, made her feel self-sufficient.

Sooner or later, though, the peaceful intermission in the stormy drama of their relationship had to end. They would have to resolve the issues that stood between them. Decide their fates, and their child's. More sooner than later, judging by the fact that he was watching her the way a hawk watched a field mouse.

Seth Evans definitely wouldn't be vulnerable much longer.

She dropped the shoes on the floor for him to step into, then held the shirt behind him and eased it up his arms and over his shoulders.

So far so good.

The buttons on the fly of his blue jeans proved more troublesome. He said nothing, just tipped his head back and stared at the ceiling while her fingers tugged and fumbled with the first two brass discs. As the third slid home, she felt a ripple in the muscles of his abdomen. Her hands automatically responded with a quaking of their own.

Breath hissed through Seth's clenched teeth. He lifted his uninjured arm, threading his hand through her hair behind her head.

Steadying himself? Or her?

Drawing in a deep breath and holding it, focused only on finishing her task, she reached for the fourth button. As her fingers worked the stiff denim, she felt the unmistakable stirring beneath. Numbness pricked at her fingertips as all her blood pooled in the center of her body.

The button escaped her. How could her core be so warm and her fingers so clumsily cold at the same time?

She grasped the brass disc again, slowly pulled it toward its slot, the growing bulge behind the denim impeding her progress. Seth's hand in her hair fisted. He pulled her up, brushed her hands away from his fly, then used his hold on her to tip her head back, bring her forward, against him.

Their bodies pressed against each other. She felt the deep rise and fall of his bare chest against her breasts. The heat of his arousal.

She froze against him for a second, too stunned to breathe. Gradually, his warmth melted her. Swallowing hard, she tried for levity. "Not bad for an injured man."

His eyelids drifted shut. "Dying man. You're killing me here, Em."

"Just how, exactly, am I doing that?" She'd never thought of herself as the femme fatale type.

His chuckle was one part laughter and three parts

groan. "Oh, I don't know. Maybe by swishing this wavy hair of yours around like an auburn ocean." As if to prove his point, he released the fist behind her head and fanned her hair over her shoulder. His hand slid down past the curve of her back. "And by sashaying this fine a—"

She spun out of his grasp. "I don't swish. Or sashay."

"The hell you don't."

"Are you saying you think I'm trying to seduce you or something?"

"No."

"Then what are you saying?"

He reached out, snagged her by a belt loop and tugged her to him. "That you're attractive. Beautiful. Even more so because you don't seem to realize it."

The rasp in his voice shot a shiver of awareness up her spine.

His gaze fixed on her mouth. "That I love the way your lips slip apart and the tip of your tongue wets them when you think I'm going to kiss you."

She clamped her mouth shut. Did she do that?

His gaze darkened, and wings of panic fluttered in her throat.

He grazed his hips against hers. "That I can't get within three feet of you without this happening. And it's damned annoying."

He didn't look annoyed. He looked...untamed. Primitively male. Dangerous.

But not annoyed.

Awed that she had put that savage look in his eyes, she felt more empowered than she had in her whole life. Never had she had such a commanding effect on a man. Control was a heady drug and it coursed through her blood until she was light-headed with it.

Self-sufficient, hell. She was master of her own fate and she planned to keep it that way. Take fate into her own two hands. Literally.

Wedging her palm between their bodies, she feathered her fingers over him. "If I'm so bothersome to have around, why don't you send me away?"

She felt the groan well up inside him before it spilled from his lips. "You know damned well why."

She palmed him, nestling her hand between his legs. "Guess you'll just have to suffer then."

A vein jumped in his neck. His hand clamped over her wrist. For a second, he pressed her closer. Then he peeled her fingers away. "You could have left anytime in the last two days."

She didn't answer the question directly. Wouldn't make it that easy on him. "I'm glad you noticed. I won't run from this fight, Seth. But don't expect me to fight fair, either. Not when you've stacked the deck against me. We're talking about my life and my *child*, here."

He jerked himself away from her, turned his back to her. "You think I don't realize that?"

"I think you realize it. I also think your heart has a few too many scars around it to care."

Marcus bellowed from the living room. "Get a move on in there, Seth, or you're going to be late."

Other than the rise and fall of his shoulders on a deep breath, Seth made no reaction to her comment. "On my way," he called to his cousin, and left without another word. A moment later, the front door opened and closed.

Emma plopped onto the edge of the bed, her knees

suddenly weak. The battle with Seth had begun, it seemed. But at least she had a new weapon. For him to react to her physically, he had to care about her on some elemental level, didn't he? His brain just hadn't figured out what his body was telling him.

The phone beside the bed clanged shrilly. Still puzzling over Seth, she picked up the portable handset. "Hello."

"Carpenter."

Her fingers tightened on the plastic casing. "Captain Yankovich."

"Go to your front window."

Nerves buzzing, she did as her superior officer ordered. Something was wrong. He wasn't supposed to contact her this way.

"See the silver sedan parked out front?"

"Yes." Dread pooled like quicksilver in her stomach. Slippery and thick.

"Get in the back. We have to talk."

Twelve

Something was dreadfully wrong. Captain Yankovich shouldn't be making contact like this. Even though Emma's cover had been blown to Seth, whoever was trying to get their hands on Stingray—and trying to kill him to do it—didn't necessarily know she was navy. Seeing her get into a government vehicle could put them all in even more danger than they were already in.

Chewing her lower lip, she slid into the back seat beside Yankovich, but left the car door open as an escape route. "Captain, this meeting is highly—"

A wide-shouldered man with burly arms climbed into the vehicle after her, pinning her between himself and Captain Yankovich. His haircut and his posture gave him away as military, despite the civilian khakis and golf shirt.

Yankovich nodded to the driver, and the electric locks thunked into place.

Emma snapped her gaze back to the captain. "What is this?"

"Nothing to worry about. We're just taking a little ride." But his rheumy eyes said otherwise. He pinched the bridge of his nose, almost sounded sorry when he said, "You're being recalled, Carpenter."

"Recalled?" Her hands fisted on her knees. She

should have expected this. She *had* expected this when she'd first disclosed her pregnancy. But not now. "Why? What's happened?"

Yankovich slanted his eyes at her sympathetically. "You know I'm not at liberty to say. My orders are to bring you back."

"I have a right to know!"

White crevices fanned out from the corners of his mouth. He turned his head and stared out the side window.

She licked her lips. "Look, I know I screwed up." No comment.

Panic rose from her gullet, choked her. "At least tell me where we're going."

"Washington," Yankovich said without looking back her way.

The Pentagon. The nerve center of naval intelligence. Whatever had happened, whatever reason they had for bringing her in, it must be big. And bad. They'd bury her so deep in the bowels of the military machine that she'd never find her way out.

And Seth would never find his way in.

This was her chance, a part of her mind encouraged. Her chance to be free of Seth, his damaged psyche and the soul-deep hurt in his eyes. To be her own person, not Seth Evans's baggage.

But no. She'd told him she wouldn't run and she'd meant it. They'd be able to work out some amicable agreement once he realized she wasn't going to steal his child. She was sure of it.

Except when he got home and found her gone, he'd think stealing his child was exactly what she had done.

She knew what that would do to him. How it would tear him up inside.

Seth.

Oh, God.

"God *bless*, Marcus!" Lurching forward in the seat of his cousin's rented Blazer, Seth clutched his injured ribs, which the doctor had poked and prodded into a raging ache. "Do you have to hit every pothole?"

"Sorry. I was distracted."

Seth followed Marcus's gaze to the blond bombshell in short-shorts and a halter top on the sidewalk. "Hey, you're a married man. A new father."

Marcus returned his attention to the road. "I said I was distracted, not pulling over to get a phone number."

Seth wiggled deeper into his leather seat and watched palm trees whip by out the passenger window. "So how do you feel?"

"I feel fine. You're the one who got thrown under the bus."

"Truck. And I went over the hood, not underneath it. I meant how do you feel about being a father."

Marcus's fingers flexed on the steering wheel. "Scariest damn thing that ever happened to me. And I been through some scary shit, you know?"

"Yeah, I know," Seth answered quietly.

"First time I saw him, though, my whole world shifted. That little wrinkled face became the center." His mouth curved in a wide smile. "And Samantha. Already fretting about losing the baby weight, 2:00 a.m. feedings and changing diapers... She's so tired she has to take a nap every afternoon just to be coherent at dinner."

"Sounds wonderful," Seth drolled.

"It is. That old cliché about motherhood is true,

man. She glows now in a way I never imagined before the baby. From the inside out.''

Seth grinned. He'd never seen Marcus so emotional. ''So do you, cousin. But in your case it's probably just because you've spent too much time on nuclear submarines.''

''Yeah, laugh now, cousin, but your time is coming soon. We'll see how funny you feel when you get your first look at your son or daughter.''

Seth sobered. A hard knot balled in his stomach. He'd almost given up thinking he'd ever have kids. With his track record with women, he hadn't been sure he'd ever be able to develop a relationship on which to build a family.

Hell. He *didn't* have such a relationship, and that thought plagued him constantly, like a splinter he couldn't quite work to the surface. All he and Emma had was one night of passion and a few weeks of shock and squabbling.

Seeing Marcus's silly grin and hearing the faraway tone in his voice when he talked about his wife and child, Seth realized he wanted more. He wanted it all—the partnership, the shared joy. The love.

There was no doubt that he and Emma were physically compatible. Maybe with time, respect and a lot of hard work they could be emotionally, too.

Seth's heart thudded painfully against his battered ribs as he realized the risk he'd be taking. For the first time in years he was actually considering letting a woman past the impenetrable wall he'd built around his heart.

Now *that* was scary.

''Home sweet condo.'' Marcus swung the SUV into a parking space outside Seth's building.

Seth's mind raced as he rode the elevator up to the eighth floor. Before he'd left, Emma had said they had a lot of things to work out between them.

He was ready to start.

He rehearsed his speech as he walked down the hall to 812 and let himself in.

"Emma?" He shut the door behind him and tossed his keys onto the spindle-legged entry table. "Em?"

Silence washed over him like a cresting wave. In a heartbeat he knew something was wrong. He limped through the dining room, the bedrooms, the baths, then back to the kitchen, anger and fear clawing at him with every step.

No note. No explanation.

No.

He pounded his fists against the refrigerator door behind him, then, ignoring the pain, slid his back down the cool metal to the floor and let his face fall into his hands.

Damn it, why had he trusted her?

She was gone, and his child with her.

Hours later Seth sat in the dark in the dining room, staring at the open bottle of bourbon and empty shot glass on the table barely visible in the moonlight angling through the window. The green numbers on the microwave clock leered at him from the kitchen—eleven-eighteen.

She'd been gone twelve hours and six minutes, assuming she'd left right after Marcus had hauled him off to the doctor this morning. Nine hours and six minutes ago, he'd accepted that she wasn't coming back. A person could run errands for two, maybe three hours. No longer. Not in Emerald Cove.

He'd expected her to run out on him sooner or later. What really bothered him was that she didn't even bother to leave a damn note. No, ''I'll send you pictures of his/her birthday parties and at Christmas.'' No, ''I'm sorry.''

No, ''Goodbye, you son of a bitch.''

Just an empty, silent apartment.

He poured two fingers of bourbon, then added a dash more for good measure. He swirled the liquid until, in the darkness, it reminded him of the sun glinting off her hair, then he slammed it back.

His throat burned, but it was nothing compared to the fire in his blood. He poured another shot.

The phone rang. He let it go until the machine answered, then swore, stalked into the kitchen and picked it up.

''Seth?''

His blood zoomed straight to boil. ''Damn you to hell.''

''Seth, please. Listen.'' Emma's voice sounded tinny and frightened.

Not quite ready to buy into whatever she was pulling, he hesitated. ''Where the hell are you?''

''At the mini-mart at Fourth and Pompano.'' Something was definitely wrong. Her voice didn't shake like that.

He squeezed the phone so hard his fingers hurt. ''Don't move. Do not move.''

''I won't.'' He heard one ragged breath, then, ''Please hurry, Seth. I'm scared.''

He was out the door before he realized he still had the portable phone in his hand. He didn't bother to take it back inside.

* * *

Emma huddled in the tiny triangle of shadow between the ice machine and the front wall of the mini-
mart, her arms clutched around herself. She didn't like
the dark. Didn't like skulking around parking lots at
midnight. But inside the twenty-four hour convenience
store she'd felt trapped. And outside, in the open,
she'd felt vulnerable.

A Greyhound bus lumbered by on Pompano Ave-
nue, belching out an acrid trail of exhaust. As it got
farther away, its red taillights seemed to watch her like
a demon's eyes.

Her knees wobbled and the muscles of her thighs
trembled from standing still so long. She wanted—
needed—to move. To pace, but she didn't dare.

They'd be looking for her by now.

A pair of headlights slashed across the front of the
store, blinding her. Emma shrank against the wall until
brick scraped her back. Her heart thundered so loud
that she thought surely the noise would give her away
to the driver. Beside her, the ice machine's motor
hummed to life. She almost yelped, thinking someone
had sneaked up behind her.

The car angled into a parking slot. The engine and
headlights cut off. Emma squinted, trying to hurry her
eyes' adjustment to the sudden dimness.

A dark silhouette, tall, rangy and male, clambered
out of a low-slung silver convertible without slowing
down to open the door. He stumbled when his feet hit
the ground, limped a step forward and clutched his
ribs as he looked around, searching the darkness.

The breath whooshed out of her. She took a tenta-
tive step into the light. "Seth. Here," she said, hardly
above a whisper.

He swooped down on her like a gull on a shiny gum

wrapper. Fury and frustration glowed in his eyes, reminding her of the bus's taillights. His hands clamped like vises on her upper arms. His breath smelled of liquor. "You promised, damn it. You promised you wouldn't leave!"

"I didn't. Not by my own choice." She glanced nervously left and right, her unease growing with every second they stood in plain sight. "Please, Seth. Could we just get out of here? I'll explain in the car."

He glared at her. For a moment she thought he would insist on getting his explanation there and then, but instead he jerked toward the car just roughly enough to let her know he wouldn't wait long.

He gave her three blocks. It was two and a half more than she expected. "Start talking, Emma. And make it a good story."

A story? Was he expecting her to lie to him?

Sure he was. He thought that was what all women did. She hadn't done much thus far to improve his perception.

She'd asked Seth to put up the convertible top and he had, but now she felt cloistered. As she fiddled with the air conditioning vent, she said, "After you and Marcus left, Captain Yankovich, my naval intelligence contact, called."

His eyes narrowed, probably at the reminder that she'd originally come to Emerald Cove to spy on him. Another example of female deception.

"What did he want?"

"He said I was being recalled."

Seth shot her a ferocious look.

Tears filled her eyes as she remembered what else Yankovich had said. Did she dare tell Seth the truth?

Or would she only be giving him the ammunition to get exactly what he wanted?

If the navy locked her up, she might never see her baby.

Then Seth would have his child.

Panic razed her already raw nerves even further. What if he wouldn't help her? What if he wanted to see her locked up, so he could take the baby?

Doubt and indecision wove a tangled trail along her neural pathways. To trust or not to trust? She didn't know. Couldn't decide, so she stalled. "You thought I ran away, didn't you?"

"What was I supposed to think? I got home and you weren't there. No note, no nothing."

"Did you even hold off on your pity party long enough to wonder whether I'd left by my own free will? Whether I might have been *forced* to go?"

He swerved the car to the shoulder of the road. "You're saying this Yankovich kidnapped you?"

She swallowed a lump the size of a conch shell. Decision time. She stared into his eyes, trying to find some glimmer of faith in her.

Then again, what did it matter if he believed her? She had nowhere else to go. No one else to turn to. At least with Seth she knew she wouldn't be in any physical danger.

"He didn't kidnap me," she told him. Her voice scratched out of a throat as dry as an old skeleton in the desert. "He arrested me."

"What the—"

"Yankovich said intelligence indicated the Rebelians might have someone on the inside at Evans Yachts. Maybe even in the navy."

She paused before she finished, but knew he'd al-

ready figured it out. It was written in the disdain on
his face.

"They think it's me. I'm the inside man." She
shook her head. "Woman."

He reached out to her in the dark. "Emma—"

She drew back, away from him. "I'm not a spy,"
she said emphatically. "I mean, I am a spy. But *for*
the U.S., not against it. I need to know you believe
that, Seth. No matter what else you believe me capable
of, I have to know you don't think I'm a traitor."

Sliding to the edge of his seat, he cupped her elbows
in his palms. She could see the battle raging inside
him. The same war between trust and mistrust she'd
just fought.

"How did you get away from them, Emma?"

"I was afraid. So I talked them into stopping at a
gas station by telling them I was sick—morning sickness. Then I lured them into the restroom. I still had
your pistol. They didn't think to search me. So I held
them at gunpoint and jammed a chair under the door.

"I pulled a weapon on my superior officer." Her
heart skipped like a flat rock over a pond. "I went
AWOL."

Finally, *finally,* he pulled her against him and
wrapped an arm over her shoulders. She burrowed
against his chest. The protective gesture wasn't the
grand profession of faith in her that she'd hoped for,
but it would do.

For now.

Seth drove in no particular direction, making ran-
dom turns and checking his rearview mirror fre-
quently. He drummed his fingers on the steering
wheel. The dashboard clock blinked 1:15 a.m.

He glanced over at Emma, slumped in her seat, shoulders rounded dejectedly. In this part of town there were no streetlights, but a three-quarter moon shone brightly, giving Emma's light complexion an opalescent sheen, except for the charcoal shadows beneath her eyes.

They were both tired. They'd have to stop soon, but where?

He couldn't take her home. With the Rebelians and now the navy after them, she wouldn't be safe there. He couldn't take her to his parents' place. Wouldn't bring this kind of trouble to his family's doorstep.

Making up his mind suddenly, he pulled a U-turn and parked in front of the Key Breeze Inn.

Emma raised her head sluggishly, as if she'd just woken from a deep sleep.

Shock, he thought. Exhaustion. And stress.

"What are we doing here?" she asked.

"Calling it a night. We both need some rest."

Less than ten minutes later they'd parked the car behind the building, where it would be less visible, and were keying open the door to unit 213. Emma walked to the sink as if she was in a trance, washed her face, then laid on the bed, her hands folded beneath one cheek.

She looked sick.

The baby...

No. Seth pushed that possibility away.

Still standing just inside the door, he scrubbed his hands over his face. "What will they do now that you've jumped ship? Send someone after you?"

"I would imagine. The navy tends to frown on desertion."

Needing to work off his restlessness, Seth paced.

Emma smiled weakly. "At least if they lock me up in Leavenworth you won't have to worry about me running off with your baby."

He wheeled, his gut contracting as if he'd been sucker-punched. "That's not funny." He sat next to her, forced himself to be gentle when he swept her wavy hair off her shoulder. "No one's locking you up anywhere." He curled one corner of his mouth. "Except me."

She didn't laugh at his joke.

"I didn't do it," she whispered instead.

"I know." How could he know with such certainty that she wouldn't betray her country, and still be so uncertain whether she would betray *him?*

He had no idea how, but he did know it. Emma Carpenter was no double agent.

She was scared.

The edge on her nerves scraped at his own uneasiness. The night's events, the worry, had left him raw. Earlier, while he'd been contemplating a good drunk, assuming she'd bugged out on him, she'd been fighting for her freedom, fighting to get *back* to him. The knowledge left him battling a bad case of the guilts, and the bitter taste of self-recrimination seared his tongue.

Right now he was more worried about her, though. She still had that faraway look in her eyes.

Tamping his inner turmoil down to a dull roar, he settled himself fully on the bed, leaned against the headboard, spread his legs and pulled her between them until her back pressed against his chest. His arms circled her waist, feeling the chill in her and the tiny tremors shivering through her muscles.

"What am I going to do?" she choked out, her tears surfacing.

He tightened his hold on her. "We'll figure something out."

"I worked hard to get in the navy." She turned her head and he caught the corner of a fierce glare. "It's not easy for a woman to get an intelligence post, you know, even as a secretary."

"I know." He didn't really, but he believed her. He glided his palm up and down the silky smoothness of her arm, calming her while he came up with a way to take her mind off her worries. "How did you end up in the navy, anyway? Seems like a long way from a pig farm in Iowa."

She sniffed, and he smiled to himself, feeling her pull herself together. "That's exactly how I ended up in the navy. I wanted to get as far away from the farm as I could." She laid the back of her head against his chest. The weight of it felt solid. Right.

"Tired of eating bacon and ham everyday?"

"Tired of always being another mouth to feed, maybe. My parents divorced when I was seven. Neither one of them really wanted me, but they didn't want the other one to have me either. So I was shuttled from house to house, farm to farm, relative to relative.

"I never had any say in where I went, whom I stayed with or how long I stayed. No matter how hard I tried to make them like me, want me, they'd eventually get tired of me and pass me on to the next kin."

He felt the painful memories shudder through her and gathered her up closer to his chest, anger burning a whole in his heart. "Terrible thing to do to a kid."

"I never blamed them. I was too much trouble. Took up too much of their time."

"You were just a child."

"I was a burden. They never asked to be saddled with me. Wouldn't have taken me if it weren't for family obligation—and the fact they'd be ashamed to show their faces at Sunday service if they turned me out. I was lucky to have a roof over my head and food in my belly."

Jesus. No wonder she'd resisted marrying him. She couldn't stand the thought of being an obligation again. A millstone weighing around someone else's neck.

"So you joined the navy to see the world."

"And earn my own way. I'll never be someone else's burden again." She craned around until she could look him in the eye. "Not even yours."

That was more like it. Now that her fighting spirit had returned, he nudged her back to the problem at hand.

He'd get back to the burden thing later.

"So what are you going to do? Run away? Live the rest of your life as a fugitive?"

"I won't let them railroad me into a court martial."

"I know you won't," he soothed. Her skin wasn't so cold under his hands anymore. In fact, a rosy flush had begun to appear.

Seth's temperature warmed a degree or two in response.

"You sound awfully sure of that for a guy who thought he could railroad me into marrying him a few days ago."

He bent his head over her shoulder and inhaled her honey and vanilla scent. "I didn't know you then."

Her head lolled to the side, giving him better access. "And now?"

"Now I've decided to change my approach." He touched the tip of his tongue to the crook of her neck, tasted the same sweetness he'd smelled. Then he hooked his left leg over hers and rolled her to the center of the bed. Supporting himself over her on his elbows, though the effort sent daggers slicing beneath his cracked ribs, he lowered his mouth to hers, not touching, just teasing.

"This is your new approach?"

"Mm-hmm." He shifted his weight to his good side and lifted his other hand to her breast. He rolled the nipple beneath her plain cotton blouse between his thumb and forefinger. "What do you think so far?"

Gasping, she arched her head back. "Could work."

With that encouragement, he let his chest sink down to hers and pinned her hands above her head. This time there was no teasing. No finesse. Just fierce desire, too long contained. Hunger.

His approach had definitely changed. He no longer cared about forcing her to marry him. Simple acquiescence wasn't good enough.

He wanted unconditional surrender.

Reaching down, he hooked one of her legs over the back of his thigh, then reared back to open the buttons on her sleeveless blouse, pausing periodically to capture her mouth in another melding, thrusting kiss. Her lips were swollen and opened to him without restraint.

Time whirled by in a flash of creamy skin, a fan of auburn hair, a shuddering moan.

Her clothes lay by the bed, a discarded tangle of cotton, denim and lace. Emma lay beneath him, around him, her breath heavy, her green eyes glazed.

Seth took a moment to drink in the sight of her. She was the most beautiful thing he'd ever seen. An ethereal creature divined of verse and rhyme in some poet's imagination.

Such perfection couldn't exist in reality.

But she was real. She was flesh and bone and blood. Quick wit and courageous heart. And she was his for the taking.

She sat up and tugged the hem of his shirt out of his pants. "Your turn."

He pushed her hands away, his brow drawing down. "No."

He couldn't do it, he realized. Couldn't take what she offered. Not after the way he'd bullied her. Not with guilt still twisted around his belly like a strand of rusty barbed wire. They had a lot to settle between them before they took that next step.

If they took the next step.

She tried to cover herself with her hands. "I—I thought you wanted..."

He rested his damp forehead against hers, reining in his raging desire. "I want. Believe me, I want." He pulled her knees up on either side of him and slid down her body. "But tonight's just for you."

Tonight he wouldn't take. He would give.

She tried to struggle away, but he stopped her with a palm on her flat belly. "Trust me?" he asked.

She swallowed. "You're the one with the trust issues, remember?"

"Right." Smiling, he lowered his head for an intimate kiss. "You're beautiful everywhere, Emma," he murmured, his breath fanning her sensitive regions. "I couldn't see you that night in the hut. Not this way. It was dark. But I knew you would be beautiful."

She bucked as he entered her with his fingers. He stilled her by nuzzling the area above his knuckles.

"Mmm. You smell good, too. And taste like... buttermilk and honey."

"Seth." It sounded as if she was talking through gritted teeth. "Please don't."

"Don't what? Do this?" He swirled his fingers provocatively, lapped at her with his mouth, kneaded and squeezed with his hand, riding the crest of the waves of pleasure tossing her hips from the coverlet.

"Yes. I mean no. I mean, please don't make me feel so...vulnerable."

He spoke to her without raising his head. "There's nothing wrong with being vulnerable, love. As long as you're with someone who will take care of you."

Her head thrashed side to side. He glanced up long enough to see her eyes were tightly shut. She was fighting it. Fighting him.

"I don't want anyone to take care of me," she panted. "I take care of myself."

Her independent streak shone through, even in this.

He took it as a challenge.

"There's nothing wrong with needing someone sometimes. With depending on someone."

"No."

"Can you do this for yourself?" Without waiting for an answer, he burrowed his face into her and suckled the center of her sexuality until she nearly floated off the bed.

Her fists clenched the bedspread, and still he pushed her farther.

He lifted her hips, driving himself farther into her. She cried out his name, and still he pushed farther.

He used more fingers, drove them harder. Hungrily, he pulled on her with his mouth until she no longer cried his name—she simply cried.

And still he pushed farther. Deeper. Inside her and inside himself. He wanted this for her. For them. The unified them—two bodies merged into one.

Opening her with his fingers, he blew his life breath on her, the way he'd blown it into her when she'd almost drowned the day the catamaran had blown up. He pressed down on her with his thumb and hoped that it would be enough. That she'd find her pleasure.

She shattered in his arms. The tremor started where he penetrated her and spiraled outward with growing strength until her arms and legs clutched at him and her fingers pulled at his hair.

He held her until the last quiver rippled out of her, then crawled up her body. She turned on her side, pillowed her head on her arm. He pulled the edge of the bedspread over her and tugged her back against his chest, where he was content to listen to her breathing gradually settle.

God, he could have lost her again today. Those navy bastards could have spirited her away and hidden her under a cloak of red tape and "national security" baloney so thick he'd have never found her.

Her, he thought, a little dizzy with the realization. It hadn't been just the thought of losing the baby that had frightened him, but the idea of never seeing Emma again.

He'd fallen in love with her.

And that scared the hell out of him.

Thirteen

Emma woke to a rustling sound. At first she thought she heard leaves rattling in the wind outside her bedroom window. Then she opened her eyes and saw Seth.

He sat, shirtless, at a small round table. His jeans were unbuttoned, as they had been yesterday. His feet were bare, his hair mussed and stubble shadowed his jaw.

It was as if the serious and somewhat arrogant CEO she'd once known had vanished, replaced by the latest scruffy but endearing Hollywood sex idol.

He grinned at her over his newspaper, the source of the rustling, and she realized she'd been staring.

"You want sports, news or comics?" he asked.

In a flash, she realized where they were. What they'd done last night.

More accurately, what *he'd* done last night. To her.

Her skin burned as if she'd fallen asleep on the beach under the midday sun. She yanked the bedspread over her head.

"I'll take that as a 'none of the above,'" Seth said mildly.

"Coffee. I want coffee."

She never heard him move, but the next thing she knew he peeled the covers back and was leering down at her.

"Me, too. But there's a bit of a dilemma where coffee's concerned. To get it, one of us would have to go out. And if we go out, we might be seen."

"No room service?"

He shook his head.

She flopped onto her back, tugged the sheet under her chin and let her arms fall spread-eagle. "What the hell were you thinking," she asked with no real malice in her tone, "checking us into a hotel with no room service?"

He grinned again. "Lost my head, I guess."

Once she'd taken a moment to pull her mind together, she sat. She put one pillow behind her and then punched the other, a tugging sensation pulling at her abdomen as the faint scents of Seth and sex wafted into the air.

Seth left the newspaper where it lay on the table, preferring instead to stand before the slight gap in the window curtains, staring out at the world with his fingertips jammed into the front pockets of his jeans.

His back was straight, his shoulders square. His feet were spread beneath a broad back and narrow hips. He looked for all the world like a man comfortable with himself. With being alone.

A man who didn't get close to people.

Especially women.

But he'd gotten close last night. Intimately close.

"I don't understand you," she said to his back.

"What's not to understand?" He shrugged. "I'm a simple guy."

With his back turned, she took the opportunity to retrieve her capris and shirt from the floor. "You're about as simple as a quadratic equation. I never know what you're thinking. Last night—"

He turned as she closed the final button on her blouse. "I'm male. Put me in a hotel room with a gorgeous woman and I pretty much only think about one thing."

The lack of meaning he gave last night stung. It would have stung more if she thought it was true.

Her back up now, she strolled up to him, holding his gaze, trying to read something—anything—in eyes the color of autumn leaves. "Just following your instincts, huh? Survival of the species. Tarzan and Jane do the monkey thing."

"Something like that."

She stopped in front of him, close enough to count each whisker. "Then why was I the only one belting out the Tarzan call?"

He broke eye contact, ducked around her, grabbed his shirt and slid it on, wincing as he lifted his arms. She waited, and he finally looked at her again.

"Maybe I just got tired of being a bully," he said.

He picked up his keys and started for the door.

"Where are you going?" she asked when she'd managed to pick up her jaw.

"To get coffee."

"I thought you were worried about being seen."

"We can't stay here without food."

"We can't stay here at all."

"You have a better idea?"

"We could try to get to one of your boats and sail to Borneo," she said without missing a beat.

He didn't look impressed. "Have you ever been to Borneo?"

"No, but it sounds exotic."

"It's a long way to go for coffee."

She took a deep breath. Time for joking was over.

In her heart, she knew what she had to do. "I don't think I have much choice but to turn myself in."

His forehead furrowed. "Forget it."

"It was crazy to run last night. I panicked."

Two strides brought him back to her bedside. An angry vein jumped on the side of his neck. "I said forget it."

She knew that look. The Hollywood idol was gone. The corporate shark was back.

"We'll find Marcus," he decided for them both. "He'll talk to the Pentagon and work it all out."

She had her doubts, but she held her tongue, as she didn't have a better plan.

It didn't take them long to find Seth's cousin.

He was waiting for them in the front seat of Seth's car.

"Geez, Seth," Marcus said, unfolding his long body from the silver Z3. "Couldn't you have gotten a car with a little more leg room?"

Seth nudged Emma behind him. "What are you doing here?" Instinctively he scanned the parking lot.

"Don't worry. I'm alone. And I'm here to keep an eye on you." He kicked a toe of his running shoe at the pavement. "Well, not *right* on you, exactly, since I'm pretty sure that whatever the two of you were doing in that room last night wasn't a matter of national security, or anything I wanted to see—"

"Marcus!" Seth cut him off.

"Anyway, I figured you couldn't leave without me if I parked myself right here."

"How did you find us?"

"I never lost you, cousin. I followed you from your condo when you picked her up last night."

Emma cocked her head. "I didn't see you."

"You're not supposed to see me, ma'am," Marcus said, dead serious. "I'm a navy SEAL."

Seth frowned as he put together the pieces to the puzzle of his cousin's behavior. Heat rose slowly up his gullet. "Why were you following me?"

Marcus's chin dropped to his chest. He heaved out a heavy breath. "Wasn't right. She was supposed to be there when you got back." When he raised his head, his expression was battle-ready, but his eyes were apologetic.

Seth didn't give a damn about his cousin's apology. He rushed him, fisting his hands in the bigger man's shirt. "You knew! You s.o.b. It was a setup all along, wasn't it? You offering to drive me to the doctor? To make sure nothing happened to me. You were supposed to make sure Emma was alone in the house so your navy pals could come calling. That's twice you've double-crossed me, you son of a bitch!"

"I didn't double-cross you. I was trying to help you."

Seth shook Marcus without releasing his hold on his cousin's shirt. Marcus didn't budge, but he didn't fight back, either.

"They said they just wanted to talk to her," Marcus complained. "They weren't supposed to take her."

"But they did take her, didn't they? Thanks to you."

"Seth," Emma said, her hand on his arm, "he was only following orders.

Seth shook her off. He wasn't in any mood for excuses.

Marcus nodded curtly. "When I heard she'd gotten

away, I figured she'd contact you, so I staked you out.''

Seth glanced around again. "So where are all your little navy buddies? Waiting behind the bushes to nab an innocent woman?''

"There's nobody in the bushes," Marcus said, and flicked Seth off like a fly. He straightened his shirt. "I don't much like being used by my own people. I came here to help, if I can. I haven't told anyone where you are.''

"It wouldn't matter if you had," Emma said stiffly. "Seth was just going to take me downtown so I could turn myself in.''

Seth growled. "Hell I am.''

Marcus shot a glance at him, then at Emma. "All due respect, ma'am, I'm with him. I don't think it'd be prudent to turn yourself over just yet.''

Seth narrowed his eyes. "What do you know?''

"Intel says there's a man inside this op.''

"It's not Emma.''

Marcus shrugged. "Which means we don't know who it is.''

"Which means we can't trust any of them," Seth said, following his cousin's thinking. He bored a hole in Emma with his glare. "No way you're going back. We've got to find someplace safe for you to wait this out.''

"You willing to let me in on this?" Marcus asked.

Seth gave him the evil eye. Marcus didn't even blink.

"You got any idea where to start?" Seth finally huffed.

"One or two. If you're of a mind to listen.''

Seth sighed. Marcus might have made a mistake,

but Seth had never known his cousin to compromise his principles. Even for the navy. And there was no one he'd rather have on his side if it came down to a fight.

"I might be," he finally said.

Marcus's shoulders relaxed a fraction. "One other thing you should know, then." He took a deep breath. "The navy's real nervous about this. They're going to take Stingray to another contractor if they don't get Emma back. If it comes down to that, you might have to choose between the sub and her."

Seth growled an oath. "If it comes down to that, it's no choice at all." His eyes burned as he looked at her, the sweet fall of curls around her face, her deep green eyes.

"I choose her."

Marcus hid Emma right under the navy's nose. He distracted his own navy watchdogs assigned to surveillance at the Faulkner house while Emma and Seth slipped in the back, then he'd come inside under the guise of visiting with Gideon.

Now they all sat in a bright yellow kitchen, shades drawn, drinking coffee and arguing about what to do next.

Marcus told Seth, "It's better if you go home and act like nothing is wrong."

"Oh, yeah," Seth answered. "That'll be believable. My fiancée disappears and I go on with business as usual."

"Fine. Gripe at the navy. File a missing persons report with the police. Just stay the hell away from Emma unless you want them to find her."

"Excuse me," Emma interjected. "What am I supposed to do, sit on my hands until you guys decide it's safe to poke my head out of my hidey-hole or I die of boredom, whichever comes first?" She looked up at Brooke and Gideon. "No offense intended."

Seth fixed a conciliatory smile on her. "We'll figure something else out, Em."

"I already have," she said.

Seth cocked his head. "I'm afraid to ask."

"I'm not," Marcus said. "Let's hear it, Carpenter."

She wet her lips, gathering her thoughts. "What we need is a misdirection. A decoy to keep the brass from skinning me while we snare the real rabbit. Seth, you have your father leak out that he's not comfortable with security at the office. He's bringing all the files home, and the rest of the work will be done from the estate. He's going to keep the plans in the most secure spot in the house, which would be..."

"The safe in his office," Seth supplied.

"The plans are to be kept in the safe, then." She turned her attention back to Marcus, who seemed absorbed in the details of her plan. "Then, Marcus, you tell the admiral you're convinced I'm not their man, but you know who is."

Marcus studied her. "So who's your decoy?"

She glanced apologetically at Brooke and her husband. "I'm sorry, Gideon. With your history with the Coalition and the World Bank Heist, you're the leading candidate to play the bad guy in this little soap opera."

Gideon grinned. "Hey, what's one more felony to a master criminal?"

"Gideon," Brooke admonished.

He winced. "Sorry."

"No," Emma said, looking at Brooke. "I'm sorry.

I hate to cause any more turmoil in your lives, but Gideon's past makes him the perfect decoy. He's a believable crook.''

She glanced quickly around the table, saw disapproval. "Sort of," she amended. "To people who don't know Gideon like we do."

Their expressions didn't change. Emma groped for a more convincing explanation. "Marcus, you could say you think it's more of the Coalition's mind control surfacing, or something."

Marcus squished up his face. "How do you know about that?"

"I have my sources." She lifted her chin. "That's why I'm in intelligence."

He stared her down.

"Okay." She shrugged. "I might have peeked inside a folder or two I shouldn't have when I was filing them."

Seth stretched his back. "Excuse me, but how does putting suspicion on Gideon take the heat off you?"

Emma poured out her plan as quickly as she'd formed it. "Marcus tells them he thinks Gideon is the inside man. He says Gideon works mostly on the stealth hull and the sub's computer systems." She looked to Gideon for acknowledgment. He nodded. "But he's been pestering Seth for the rest of the components. The integrated plans—engines, weapons, navigation.

"Marcus says he's worried Gideon may be reacting to some more garbage planted in his mind, but he needs me to prove it. Marcus also says he doesn't know where I am, but that Seth does, and that Seth has agreed to cooperate as long as he gets assurances I won't be hauled off to the dungeon or anything."

She took a deep breath, let her rapt audience digest that much before continuing. "When they ask why you need me in order to catch Gideon, you say that Gideon doesn't get out of the house much."

"True again," Gideon said.

"But he won't turn down an invitation to—" she looked at Seth "—our wedding. Which will be held at the Evans's estate. Where Seth's father just happens to be keeping all the Stingray plans."

She saw the jolt pass through Seth, the questions flood his eyes. There would be time to answer them later. If she had any answers.

Marcus rolled his tongue around his cheek. "Word gets to Gideon that's where the plans are, they'll figure he won't be able to resist making a play during the wedding."

"That's what I'm hoping," Emma said. "It'll have to be a big wedding. Lots of commotion. Lots of people milling around to make the bad guy feel comfortable. Plus, we want to make sure our bad guy doesn't have any trouble getting in. When the brass starts to squabble, Marcus, you tell them not to worry. You'll have Seth move the plans on the day of the wedding. Replace them with a gibberish copy and put the real ones in the second most secure place in the house. Where would that be?"

Seth thought. "No place special in the house. But there's a safe on Pop's yacht."

"The *Pisces* it is, then. That's even better, since it's away from the house."

Marcus smiled. "So while the cats are all lined up waiting for the mouse to steal the cheese out of Russell's safe—"

"The real villain—if there really is a mole in the

navy—will go for the yacht,'' Brooke Faulkner finished, clasping her hands in front of her gleefully. She was quick.

"Where Marcus and Drew and Holt and anyone else we know can be trusted will be waiting.'' Pleased with herself, Emma smiled.

"How soon do you think we could pull this together?'' Gideon asked her.

"How's Saturday?''

Seth's forehead wrinkled worriedly. "I don't know, Em. It's a good plan, but there's still a lot that could go wrong.''

"Have you got a better idea?''

Silent, Seth dragged a hand across the back of his neck.

"Well, then.'' Marcus clapped and rubbed his hands together. "The only question that leaves is who's going to tell Aunt Lynn she has three days to plan a wedding.''

"Dahling.'' Bridget Vaughn whisked into Seth's office doing her best Eva Gabor imitation.

Out of spite, Seth kept his eyes on his desk, making her wait until he was ready to acknowledge her presence. He was still ticked at her for breaking Emma's pregnancy in her column.

"Oh, Seth.'' The fake accent vanished. "Don't be so petty. How was I to know that your fiancée hadn't told you she was pregnant?''

She caught on quick.

Reluctantly, Seth raised his head. "You might have asked, Bridget. Better yet, you might have left private business private instead of splashing it across the news.''

At least she had manners enough to look sorry.

"Now what do you want?" he grumbled.

"You summoned me, as if you didn't know it."

Raising one eyebrow, he acted as if he didn't remember. "Did I?"

"Enough, already. Consider me flogged and hung from the yardarm, or whatever it is you seamen do."

A grin tugged at the corner of his mouth despite himself.

"I need a favor, Bridge, and don't give me any grief. You owe me one and you know it." He saw the glint in her eye and continued. "I want you to run a story on my wedding."

She crossed her legs sinuously. "What makes a simple wedding newsworthy?"

"It won't be a simple wedding. It's being held at the estate, and my mother is planning it." He knew she wouldn't miss the implications of that statement. The estate was palatial by some standards, and his mother didn't do anything second-rate. "And I need the publicity. I want everyone I know in Emerald Cove to come, but I don't have time for invitations. We're doing this on Saturday."

"Seth, that's the day after tomorrow. I have deadlines—"

"You can pull it off."

Her mouth hung open, flabbergasted. "Did you say you want *everyone* to come?"

"Everyone who can scrounge up a wedding gift." He rolled his pen across his desk. "Kidding. What do you say? Will you do it?"

She cut her eyes sideways at him. "Can I stop by this afternoon for a few shots of the estate to run with the copy?"

"I suppose." The Evans's estate was like the Graceland of Emerald Cove. People were curious about it.

"A few shots of the bride and groom?"

"Don't push your luck."

When Bridget was gone, Seth walked toward the executive restroom attached to his office. Emma stepped from behind the door.

"What do you think?" he asked.

"I think that woman wants you."

He laughed, and swept her hair behind one delicate ear. "Tough. I'm taken."

Her smile faltered. "Seth, this wedding is just for show, right? It's not real."

His mood darkened as if a cloud had parked itself over his head. "It could be." He cupped the back of her neck in his palm. "Or not."

"Seth," she said. Her eyelids flitted shut.

He pulled his hand away, turned and headed back to his desk to keep himself from touching her again. "I know, I know. We have a lot to work through before we do anything permanent."

She eased over to him and propped her hip on the desk. "Our emotions are running high right now. We're both wound up, caught in this crazy scheme. Neither of us is in any frame of mind to make a life-altering decision."

"Yeah, sure. You're right." He bent over his work so she wouldn't see the lie in his eyes, but couldn't keep the hurt from his voice. She was like a mouse in a cage, so afraid of being cornered that she couldn't stop running, never realizing that she was running on an exercise wheel, never getting anywhere.

Regardless of what she thought of his state of mind, he knew exactly what he wanted.

Now all he had to do was convince her that she wanted it, too.

Fourteen

Emma couldn't believe she was getting married in fourteen hours. Not for real, she reminded herself. This wedding was all icing and no cake, one might say.

She'd come to think of it as a trial run if she decided to marry Seth.

Lord, she couldn't believe she was even considering it.

She wouldn't consider it. Not until this whole double-agent business was settled.

At least she didn't have to hide out at cheap hotels anymore. Marcus had presented their sting idea to the navy powers-that-be and gotten grudging approval. She could show her face in public without fear of being hauled off to Leavenworth.

For the time being, at least.

"Emma, this is Jean-Pierre." At the sound of Mrs. Evans's voice, Emma turned to find herself staring at the chest of a very tall man. He had to be six foot five. When she tilted her head back she could see that his head was cue ball bald and his face slightly pocked, but he had a nice smile.

Mrs. Evans beamed at her as she shook Jean-Pierre's hand. "Jean is a pastry artist. He's the Picasso of pastry."

She pumped the chef's lily-soft hand even as her cheeks ached from her forced smile. Over the past two

days, Mrs. Evans had towed a flotilla of florists and
caterers and gardeners and decorators past her. She'd
smiled ingratiatingly at each one and listened to the
conversations between them and her pretend future
mother-in-law, but she still didn't know a canapé from
a calla lily.

Thank goodness she didn't have to. Mrs. Evans
seemed to have the wedding details well in hand, leaving Emma free to concentrate on catching a traitor.
Which reminded her it was about time to find Seth
and see how the security preparations were coming.

She excused herself, leaving Mrs. Evans and Jean-
Pierre discussing raspberry tarts. As she walked in the
room they'd designated security central, Seth looked
up from a black-and-white monitor displaying Russell
Evans's office. From the number of similar monitors
lining the folding table, they had the better part of the
house wired. "Hey," he called, glancing over his
shoulder at her. Even that short look contained power.
Heat.

The region below her stomach rumbled in response.
"Hey yourself. How's it going?"

"Take a look-see." He stepped back to give her a
clean view.

A hand waved across the monitor. Holt's voice
crackled out of a walkie-talkie on the table. "Video
check, camera four."

Seth picked up the portable radio and answered.
"Camera four, looking good."

"Impressive," she said. "Have you got all the crit-
ical areas covered?"

He played with the switches on a complicated control panel. Each of the monitors came on in turn, then

off again. "Meet me in the garden later tonight and I'll show you."

A warning hum buzzed deep inside her. The question had been too smooth. As if it had been practiced.

"Why the garden?"

He shrugged. "Thought we might take a walk. We could both use a little quiet time before the big day tomorrow."

The hum in her blood became a shriek. Out of deference to his parents, she and Seth hadn't been sharing a room at night. An arrangement she was sure Seth wasn't too fond of. "Quiet time, huh?"

He slapped the monitor switches off. "Look, it's just a walk. If you don't want to go, all you have to do is say so." He wheeled and headed toward the door.

"Wait. I—" If they were ever going to find peace, she had to stop questioning his motives at every turn. "A walk sounds nice."

"Ten o'clock, by the fountain?"

She clasped her hands behind her, suddenly shy under the intensity of his scrutiny. "Ten o'clock."

At nine fifty-eight, Seth sat down on the stone wall surrounding the garden fountain on his parents' terrace. He tapped his feet and fretted with the single lily he'd brought her. The gurgling water at his back did little to settle his nerves. Hearing Emma's light footfalls, he jumped to his feet.

Before she turned the corner around the end of the hedge, he combed his hair back, wishing it would hurry up and dry. Damn humidity. He'd showered and shaved, brushed his teeth and changed his clothes.

Still, he was absolutely certain he'd forgotten something. Like pants.

Geez, he was nervous as a teenager on prom night.

He was looking down, reassuring himself he'd remembered pants, when she turned the corner.

She was the one who'd forgotten her pants, he thought when he lifted his head. She'd put on a dress, a white flowing thing that dipped low between her breasts and swirled around her thighs like ribbon.

"Hey," she said, stopping in front of him.

He tried to say "hey" back, but found he'd lost the power of speech.

"This for me?" She took the lily from his hands, sniffed it. "Nice."

Reverently, he fingered the shoulder of her dress. "Not as nice as this."

She held her arm out to him. "You promised me a walk."

"So I did." He hooked his arm in hers and strolled past the fountain, through the arrangements of potted palms and sculptured holly shrubs.

Gradually the sounds of the house faded behind them. The lights dimmed and there was only him and Emma and the moonlight and the sound of waves slapping the beach. The night was perfect for a relaxing, romantic stroll, and yet he could feel the tension in her.

"Guess everything's ready for tomorrow," she said. Her voice sounded jittery.

"Think so."

He turned them toward the docks. Pampas grass waved along the path, mixed with thin, low-lying ferns that made the air at ankle level feel cooler somehow.

"Tell me something about yourself, Em," he suggested.

"Like what?"

"Anything. I'd like to know the woman I'm going to marry tomorrow a little better."

She stopped and quirked an eyebrow at him. "The woman you're going to *pretend* to marry tomorrow. If we get that far before somebody makes a run on Stingray."

He inclined his head in assent.

She walked off again, her step unhurried. She treaded a few feet forward, then sighed. "I've told you about my past. You know why I don't feel right about marrying you."

He shrugged. "I figured it was because I pretty much blew the proposal."

"Well, there is that, too," she said dryly, then grinned at him.

They stepped onto the pier. He pulled her to his side until their hips bumped with each step. "You told me all the bad stuff about your childhood. Tell me something good. Something I would never guess about you."

She walked absently for a few strides, as if her thoughts drifted on a gentle current. "You know that for the first seventeen years of my life I felt like I was always in the way. Useless and underfoot. I was incredibly lonely. What you don't know is that to entertain myself, I used to make up stories in my head for hours on end. Sometimes the characters felt more real to me than my family. I still daydream, sometimes. Make up my stories."

"Tell me about them."

"You wouldn't want to know. They're childish."

"I won't laugh. I promise."

She looked at him sideways. "The usual. You know, princes and damsels in distress. Fairy tales. Sometimes spy stuff, but that one's gotten a little too realistic lately."

"Do I ever show up in these fairy tales of yours?"

"You might have made an appearance or two."

That small confession pleased him inordinately. "Sounds like your active imagination helped you get through some tough times as a kid. Nothing wrong with that. You're a survivor."

"Yes, I survived. But not unscathed. I learned to loathe being dependent on other people. People who don't really want me."

He wondered if she realized her fists were clenched. He carefully unwound her fingers and held her hand while she boarded the *Pisces*.

"I hate feeling like excess baggage," she said, standing on the polished deck. "A burden."

He stopped her at the stairs that led to the stateroom below. He turned her toward him, wouldn't let her look away. "What would it take to convince you that you're not a burden to me?"

Unshed tears shimmered in her eyes. "You want a baby. I'm just the vessel to carry it for you."

His hand on her jaw shook with barely controlled fury. He wanted to rage at her, shake her, scream.

Instead he stroked her bowstring lips with his thumb. "Damn," he whispered hoarsely. He let his hand fall away from her face, took her hand and tugged gently. "I can't do this. Let's go back to the house, talk about these self-esteem issues of yours."

Her cheeks flushed. "I don't have self-esteem issues."

"Honey, any woman as intelligent and beautiful and good-hearted as you who thinks she's just a *vessel* has enough self-esteem issues to sink a barge."

She made the clucking sound seriously ticked off women make and yanked her hand out of his. She turned toward the hatch.

"Don't—" he warned.

Too late.

He followed her into the cabin, wincing as her head swiveled, taking it all in. Dozens of lilies matching the one in her hand sprang from vases, were scattered on chairs and countertops, floated in broad pans of scented water. Muted light from brass sconces blended with candlelight from the fat wax pillars sprinkled among the lilies to bathe the room in a warm glow. A piano concerto tinkled softly from a hidden sound system. A bottle of chilling wine served as the centerpiece atop a massive wooden dining table.

"You—" She spun slowly around, her eyes wide. "You did all this?"

"All by my lonesome." He decided to uncork the wine. He needed a drink.

"Why?"

He didn't deign to answer that. She was a big girl; she'd figure it out.

"Seth." Her touch shocked his back. He nearly dropped the wine. "It's beautiful," she said.

"It's…a mistake."

"Because you've suddenly decided I have low self-esteem?"

"Because we're in a Catch-22. The harder I try to get you to marry me, the more you'll believe it's only because I want my baby." He trailed a finger over her belly, felt her shiver in response. "And the more you

resist marrying me the more I'm sure it's because
you plan to run off with my child, so the more com-
pelled I feel to get a ring on your finger at any cost.
Catch-22. You want some wine?''

He didn't wait for her answer. He poured one glass
to the brim and a splash in the other. He held that one
out to her.

She splayed her fingers over her abdomen. Over
their child. ''I can't have alcohol.''

''A sip won't hurt you.''

She took the glass, but toyed with it instead of
drinking. The tip of one finger circled the crystal rim.
''So you're saying we're both letting our insecurities
doom us to a life of unhappiness and uncertainty.''

''Not a very flattering picture of either one of us, is
it?''

''No.''

He drained his wineglass. The alcohol warmed a
trail to the pit of his stomach, where it sat in a heavy
pool. Emma tasted her drink then set her glass aside
and walked toward him in a slow, considering stride.
Her hips swayed and her shoulders rolled gently with
each step.

Seth's body leaped to attention under her perusal.
His gaze locked on to hers. He could no more have
torn it away than he could have torn off an arm.

When she reached him, she took the empty glass
from his numb fingers and set it on the end table. Like
a kid who'd sneaked into his first adult movie, he
could only watch in rapt fascination, wondering what
would happen next.

''Prove it,'' she said softly.

He blinked. ''What?''

''I don't like being a slave to my insecurities. Prove

the baby isn't the only reason you want to marry me.''
Her emerald eyes darkened to deep forest green. She
lifted his hand to her chest, curled it against herself.
"Make love to me, Seth. Make love to me like you
mean it.''

Shock slammed into him like a twenty-foot breaker.
His heart stopped, restarted in a rat-a-tat-tat beat. His
first instinct was to throw her over his shoulder and
carry her to the stateroom before she changed her
mind. Instead he asked, ''Are you sure?''

She shook her head slowly. ''I'm sure I'm scared
to death. And probably the biggest fool in the world
for considering this, but I have to *know*. Words can
lie. Actions can't. Hearing you tell me you want me—
just for me, not because of the baby—isn't good
enough. I need you to show me how you feel.''

Seth didn't need to hear any more. He scooped her
off her feet. He'd show her how he felt about her. All
night long.

But not here, on the hard floor. He wanted a bed
for her, with soft pillows and cool sheets.

Stumbling against the rush of desire, the craving, he
headed for the stateroom. Halfway there, she threaded
her fingers through the hair at his nape and curled her
tongue over his earlobe. Praying for strength, he
charged across the last six feet of main cabin. Outside
the door to the private quarters, he fell forward, pinning Emma between his chest and the wall.

His mumbled apology was lost in the depths of her
sweet mouth. Shifting her so that her back was square
against the wall and his hips split her legs, he coaxed
her lips apart, thrust his tongue inside and drank from
her like a man dying of thirst. She tasted of cinnamon
mints and the wine she'd sipped earlier.

Her legs wound around his trunk, heels grinding into the backs of his thighs. "Seth," she gasped when he finally gave her a chance to breathe. "I can't wait. Now. Here."

She rocked against him. He almost burst right then. She was driving him crazy. He couldn't wait, either.

"No," he growled, reining in his thundering need. He remembered the soft pillows and cools sheets.

Using his foot, he pushed open the door to the stateroom, where a king-size bed with a white comforter floated on a sea of plush, midnight blue carpeting. A single palm frond adorned the center of the comforter.

Still in his arms, Emma leaned down to brush her fingers of the stem. "What's this?"

Seth cut his eyes away, suddenly embarrassed at his sentimentality. "Feeling nostalgic, I guess."

Her darkened eyes turned soft and doelike. "The pallet we made on the island."

Embarrassment hardened into determination. "We weren't worried about our insecurities there, Emma. It was just you and me, and it was good. It'll be good again."

Smiling almost imperceptibly, she toyed with the sparse hair beneath the open vee of his shirt collar. "You were about to prove that to me, remember?"

He shoved the palm to the foot of the bed and laid Emma on her back. Slowly he walked his hands forward until his hips settled on top of hers, then his chest. He supported most of his upper-body weight on his elbows, leaning on her just enough to create a tingling friction between them with each laborious breath.

Like that, he waited, giving his libido time to fall to a manageable level and working out his strategy.

"Are you all right?" she asked after several moments of silence and stillness.

He nodded. "Just figuring out how to show you how I really feel about you without sending you running out of the room, screaming in terror."

"I doubt it could be that horrifying."

She squirmed, and involuntarily he ground himself against the juncture of her thighs. Let her feel the hard truth behind his words. "Honey, you have no idea the things I want to do to you. With you."

Her eyes widened. Her lips parted. Seth took that as an invitation and captured them in another kiss, once again plunging his tongue deep inside, taking her mouth the way he wanted to take her body, but wouldn't allow himself. Not yet.

When he raised his head, she gazed at him dazedly and whispered, "Tell me what you want to do to me."

Another burst of desire exploded in him at the contrast of the virginal way she pulled her lower lip shyly between her teeth and her blatantly sexual request. With some difficulty, he drew in a cooling breath and let it out slowly before leaning down and murmuring a few suggestions in her ear.

"Oh…"

Smiling at her surprise, he slithered down her body, shoved her slinky dress up over her hips, then sat her up long enough to pull the clingy material over her head and toss it aside. What lay underneath took his breath away. He eased her gently back to the mattress, devouring her with his eyes the way he intended to devour her with every other part of his body in a few moments.

The white silk bra was low cut. Lacy scallops arced along the edge of cups so thin they were transparent.

Dusky aureoles and peaked nipples begged for his touch. He accommodated, taking first one and then the other in his mouth, fondling, suckling, cherishing.

When the flimsy material was soaked with his own moisture and Emma lay writhing in pleasure, he took it off of her and moved lower. The matching panties were a French design—cut high and narrow on the thigh, riding low on her flat abdomen. He laved her through them, liking the feel of the silky-soft fabric on his tongue. Liking the feel of the hot, moist flesh beneath even better.

Emma arched off the bed, offering herself to him, and he took her. Gliding the fragile scrap of material down her long legs, he left a trail of kisses from her hips to her ankles. She pulled him up when he'd finished undressing her, started unbuttoning his shirt.

"No." He pushed her hands away. "I'm the one with something to prove, remember."

He lowered her to her back and called on every scrap of knowledge he had about pleasing a woman to show Emma how he felt about her. How beautiful she was. How important. How he wanted to give her tonight, tomorrow, and all his tomorrows after that.

He murmured his encouragements.

She whimpered her pleasures.

With his hand between her legs he drove her upward; with his teeth on her breast he held her down. He pushed her to one precipice, tossed her over the edge, then dragged her up and over another. When his fingers entered her a third time, stretching and searching for erogenous zones, she gasped for him to stop.

"I can't…can't take anymore."

He gave her no respite, propelling her relentlessly, unforgivingly to the brink of another orgasm.

She could take. She could take, and take, and take until he had no more to give.

He went suddenly still, his pulse tripping.

She hadn't really taken anything. Not herself. Oh, she'd let him know that she wanted him, but as soon as she'd given the okay, he'd taken control.

It all came down to control, didn't it?

As a child she'd had none. She'd been forced to accept whatever someone else was willing to give. Despite her self-proclaimed need for independence, she was still accepting the scraps someone else threw her.

He threw her.

She'd never really learned to take control. To fight for what she wanted. Until she did, she'd always be someone else's burden.

Though the need to drive himself into her threatened his resolve, his sanity, he held himself back.

"Seth?" She clawed at his shoulders as if hanging on to the edge of a cliff by her fingernails. "Seth, please."

Getting no response, she bucked her hips against his. He reared back, denying her the friction she sought, and held her thrashing head still with a hand under her jaw. The glazed eyes that looked up at him were heavy-lidded. Barely coherent.

"Please, what?" he asked, steeling himself against the confusion, the urgent need twisted into her delicate features.

"Please don't stop. I need you."

"How bad? How much do you need me?"

"I—" she mewled, swallowed hard. "I need you so bad I can't breathe. Why are you doing this?"

"You wanted to know how I felt," he said. "Now you know."

He shoved himself off the bed, stood with his back to her. "I don't want to want you, just like you don't want to want me right now. Sometimes I don't even like myself for wanting you. But there you are. And the need swells in my chest until I can't breathe, just like you."

He heard the covers rustle behind him, and in a moment she stormed past him, wearing the bedspread like an oversize bathrobe. She tripped on the edge as she passed, and he caught her by the wrist, held her to him. Her eyes burned with fury.

"Don't tell me you don't feel the same way," he said. "Don't tell me you don't feel this connection between us. It's primitive and it's painful and it's damned irritating, but it's here." He thumped his chest with his fist, then tapped her between her breasts, softening his voice. "And it's here. I know you feel it."

"The only thing I feel at the moment is used."

"Then use me back. You're the one who wants to be so independent. Don't wait for me to give you what you need. Take it!"

Her eyes widened. Her nostrils flared. She jerked her wrist out of his grasp, her face twisting in rage. For a moment he thought she would run, after all.

Instead she gripped either side of his shirtfront and ripped. Buttons popped free and scattered on the floor. She yanked the shirt down his back, but not completely off, binding his hands behinds him, snared in the cuffs.

Both breathing heavily, they stared at each other for several long seconds.

"Don't stop now," Seth finally said. "It's just getting interesting."

She grabbed his head in both hands, raised up on

her tiptoes and kissed him. Hard. Behind him, his hands clenched into fists as he resisted the urge to tear free of the shirt.

She needed to feel in control, he realized. He'd nearly pushed her too far. Nearly lost her. Now he had to let her find herself, even if it killed him.

She massaged his nipples, drawing a groan from his gut, then fell to her knees to work on his belt buckle. Her makeshift robe fell around her in a pool of white down.

Seth gritted his teeth as she caressed him. Kissed him. Took him with her mouth. His head tipped back. Something akin to a feral growl crawled up his throat and out of him.

This wasn't what he expected of her. What he wanted for her. But he let her have her way. Let her take him further than he'd allowed any other woman, fighting the instinct to rip free of his restraints and take her to the floor every second.

This was her show. She was in control.

He rode a peak of pleasure so intense it bordered on pain. His fists clenched behind his back until his fingers were numb. The cords of his neck strained against the restraint of his skin. He was about to explode when she rocked back on her heels and smiled up at him.

"Had all you can take, big guy?"

He closed his eyes and moaned at the gleam in her green eyes. He'd created a monster.

"Me?" The single syllable took every bit of breath he had. His chest heaved before he could continue. "I'm just getting warmed up."

He found himself falling backward onto the carpet, Emma plastered to his chest, even before he finished the sentence. His shirt ripped, freeing one arm momentarily. She distracted him with a kiss and used the remnant to bind his wrists to the leg of the bed over his head.

So much for soft pillows and cool sheets. Thick carpeting and a bunched-up comforter would have to do. The hunger was too deep, too urgent to wait. She came down on top of him, filling herself with him, surrounding him with her hot, slick body. Time paused for the span of a glance.

She smiled. He nodded. Time restarted in fast forward. Seconds, minutes—hours, for all he knew— spun by in a blur of urgent touches, panted breaths and slick friction as she pumped herself up and down his shaft, taking what she needed from him.

Release closed in on him like fog around a boat at sea. He staved off the explosion as long as he could, sweat beading at his brow and dripping into his eyes, fingernails digging into his palms above his head.

Emma erupted first. Her face went slack, almost peaceful for a second, then tensed as the convulsions at her core spiraled outward. Her spasms gripped him, milked him. The ripple effect drove him past the point of control.

Shouting her name hoarsely, blind with the intensity of his climax, he pulled his hands out of their restraints, held her hips down and thrust up one last time.

When the gray world resolved once again into shapes and colors, Emma lay curled on his chest. She purred, but the rumbling reminded him more of a sleeping lioness than a kitten.

He questioned her by raising one eyebrow. One was all he could manage.

"Just in case I haven't made it clear," she replied, "when I want something—really want it—there's no confusion about it. No angst over not wanting to want it, or not liking myself for wanting it." She bit his chin, then released. "I take it."

"Uh, I think you made that pretty clear." He gathered her in his arms, pulled his head back and squinted at her out of one eye. "When did my quiet, competent little secretary become so completely terrifying?"

"Somewhere between being blackmailed into marrying her boss and going AWOL from the navy, I think."

He laughed, the first full, rich humor he'd felt in he couldn't remember how long. "I guess that would do it."

Tucking her head in the crook of his neck, he laid his head back and closed his eyes. This night hadn't turned out anything like he'd planned—nothing ever did with Emma, it seemed—Lord knew what tomorrow would bring.

Tomorrow.

A cloud of doubt darkened his mood. Tomorrow he was opening his family's home to an attempted murderer. A traitor. Maybe even a terrorist. He was inviting him to mingle with family and friends. To witness the wedding.

Emma's wedding.

Fear struck him deep and hard. He was putting her in harm's way, and for what? A submarine?

Emma was the best, most beautiful, most precious thing in his world. Nothing was worth risking her for—not Stingray, not Evans Yachts. Not his own life.

The irony that tonight he had finally made progress on convincing her to stay with him of her own free will twisted through him like a corkscrew.

Because tomorrow he had to send her away.

Fifteen

A dazzling morning sun winked over the rim of the porthole over Emma's head. Outside, an unseen gull cawed for its breakfast.

Emma crouched on the mauve tile floor of the *Pisces* head, leaned over the toilet and wretched. She'd been in here since dawn—nearly half an hour ago—and her stomach had yet to stop turning itself inside out every forty-five seconds or so.

Rather than complain, Emma smiled. She balanced herself against the john with one hand and laid the other over her churning stomach. Despite the discomfort, she was relieved at this first physical sign of her pregnancy. Until now, she'd had only her doctor's word that she carried a child. Now the little being inside her was making his or her presence known. In a big way.

She clutched her middle and gagged again. She heard a shuffling from the stateroom. In the mirror over the sink, she saw the brass knob behind her rotate. The door clicked open.

Seth's sleepy eyes jolted to full wakefulness. He fell to her side, one arm over her shoulders, another supporting her underneath. "God, Emma. Are you hurt? Did you fall? What happened?"

"Sick," she managed to say, grimacing.

He jumped to his feet, wet a washcloth and pressed

it to her forehead. "I'm sorry, Em. I forgot about the seasickness. I didn't think."

"Not seasick. Baby sick."

"The baby?" Placing her hand under his to hold the compress, he left her again, his movements jerky, almost panicked. "Stay put. Stay calm. I'll get a doctor."

She barely managed to stop him before he was out the door. "Seth."

He turned back, brown eyes swirling with worry. "Do you need an ambulance?"

"No ambulance."

"Are you sure?"

"Seth, I'm sure. Calm down."

"Calm down? You're sick. The baby—" His hand scratched over his stubbly cheek and through his mussed hair.

"The baby is the reason I'm sick, sweetheart."

"You could be—" He paused, looked thunderstruck. "Morning sickness?"

She nodded.

He crouched beside her again. Delight twinkled in his golden brown eyes. The corners of his mouth twitched.

"It's okay," she said grudgingly. "You can smile."

His instantaneous grin nearly swallowed his face. "How's it feel?"

"What kind of stupid question is that?" she snapped without any real ire. She was grinning too. "It feels...sick."

He touched her cheek so tenderly it brought tears to her eyes. "Oh, boy," he said. "Here come the mood swings, too."

"Laugh and you're a dead man."

"Wouldn't dream of it," he chuckled, holding up his hands.

She wretched again, mortified. But instead of being grossed out, he held her hair back. It was the sweetest thing she could ever remember anyone doing for her. This time when the tears came, they came full force.

He pulled her against him, let the saltwater run down his chest. "Why don't you come back to bed and lie down?"

"Can't," she sniveled.

"I'll bring you a bucket or something."

She glanced at the rising sun. Her stomach lurched, this time for an entirely new reason. Leaning heavily on Seth, she wobbled to her feet and wiped her face with the back of her hand and swished some water through her mouth at the sink. "I've got too much to do. I'm getting married in a few hours."

She was going to go through with it. Not just the pretend wedding, but a real one. She wasn't sure exactly when she'd decided that, but the decision left her lighter. Freer. Last night Seth had convinced her that she meant something to him. And to be honest, she was happy she'd have him nearby while she carried and birthed his baby. With this morning's confirmation of the presence of a little life inside her came another, less satisfying realization.

She was scared.

She didn't want to go through pregnancy and childbirth alone. She needed Seth's strength.

He helped her to bed. She lay down, thinking she'd rest for just a minute. Seth spooned himself behind her. His warmth seeped through her, and she suddenly realized they were both naked. Judging by his state of arousal, she guessed he'd realized it some time ago.

"Sorry, pal," she said. "I don't think I'm in any shape."

"Give it a minute," he grumbled in her ear. "It'll go away."

She wiggled, burrowing deeper into his embrace and giggling when her antics drew a groan out of him. "Oops," she said, her nausea fading.

"Uh-huh," he said suspiciously.

Her giggle burst into a laugh. "Geez, listen to us. We sound like an old married couple." She turned to face him, careful not to create any more friction than necessary. "We will be an old married couple soon. We're going to do it, aren't we? Get married for real. Try to make this relationship work."

He tensed. "We need to talk about that."

"Not getting cold feet are you?" she joshed.

His mouth set in a grim line. Her heart thudded in a lopsided beat.

"You are getting cold feet!" She sat up, clutching the sheet to her bare breasts. What had she done wrong? Had she been too aggressive last night? Displeased him some way? He'd seemed satisfied enough at the time.

"It's not what you think, Emma."

"You were the one who wanted to get married. You blackmailed me, remember?"

He sat up, also, not bothering to cover his stiff, naked sex. "I remember. But this whole phony wedding thing is just a bad idea."

"I can't believe this." She scrambled off the bed, taking the sheet with her, but he was sitting on one corner of her makeshift toga. He used it to reel her back to him.

"I'm worried about you, Em. This setup is crazy.

We don't know who's going to show today, or how far they'll go to get their hands on Stingray. I'm trying to protect you."

"Maybe I don't want to be protected. I know my career is a little tenuous right now, but I am still in the navy. I have a job to do—and it includes catching whoever is trying to steal your precious submarine plans."

"Forget it. You're going back to Maryland or Iowa or wherever the hell you're from. Take a vacation. Visit your family."

Visit her family? Hadn't he been listening to her? With her family was the last place she wanted to be.

She needed to be somewhere she was wanted. Needed. She'd thought that somewhere was here, with him.

Obviously she'd been wrong.

"No."

"Damn it! This guy nearly killed you once already. I'm not giving him another chance to hurt you. Or our baby."

"Liar," she snarled. She poked his chest with her index finger, reading the truth in the way he avoided her gaze. "This isn't about me or my baby. You're trying to keep your precious ego safe. I got to you last night, didn't I? I broke through your thick, indifferent hide, and now that you've had time to think about what a real marriage, not some hostage deal you control, will mean, you're scared."

She tugged once more on the sheet. When he tugged back, she let go of it. White percale fluttered to the floor like a settling swan.

"You can back out of the wedding if you want," she said, pulling her back straight and reminding herself that she had never wanted to get married in the first place. "But I'm not leaving. Not until we've caught whoever's after Stingray."

She'd almost made her way out the door when he jerked her back by one wrist. Before she could regain her balance, he slammed her back against the wall, pinned her in place with hands on either side of her head.

"Don't test me on this, Emma. I want you to leave."

"Even poor little rich boys don't always get what they want. I'd have thought Tiffany taught you that. Did she really run away with her son, or did you drive her off, like you're trying to do to me?"

She surged forward, taking advantage of his momentary shock and the disabling pain that scrolled across his face. Refusing to regret using his love for a child against him, she gained an inch of space between her back and the wall.

He shoved her back in place. "Don't play with me, Emma."

"Then don't lie to me. Or to yourself. You can't deny you still want me." She glanced at the evidence standing upright between their bodies.

"You want honesty? How about this?" He wedged a knee between her thighs, followed it with his hand. His thick fingers probed, found the inflamed bud of her desire.

"Don't," she moaned. But her arms clutched him closer.

"You're as ready as I am," he said, his breath hot against the side of her neck. "What does that say about us, that we can be so angry and so aroused at the same time?"

"It's a—" She gasped as his fingers drove deeper. She couldn't have stopped her hips from gyrating over him if she'd tried. "It's a purely physiological reaction."

"Uh-huh. Like the release of adrenaline and a pounding heart. There's fine line between sex and violence, Emma. Want to cross it together?"

"No."

"Now who's lying? Your mouth is saying *no,* but your body's begging for it, baby."

She didn't bother to deny it.

He let go of her with one hand, pressed her breast up toward his mouth. His teeth closed over her nipple, tugged. She felt the pull all the way to her womb.

"You're not going to scare me into running away."

"No, you're not afraid of anything, are you?" He pressed the tip of himself inside her. "Not the U.S. Navy. Not the Rebelians. Especially not me."

He pulled back, and she clasped herself around him, frantically trying to hold him in place until he surged into her again, began a pounding rhythm. Hooking her legs around his hips, she met every thrust.

"Well, I am," he said hoarsely, driving into her hard enough to bang her shoulders against the wall. "I'm afraid. Of losing you."

Her breath stuttered in her throat. She reached out to touch his face but he reared back, his eyes haunted, hollow. "I love you, damn it. Is that what you wanted to hear? I love you so damn much it hurts, and I'm afraid you're going to rip my heart out for it."

Love? He *loved* her?

Oh, God.

Silently, she pulled him into her, with her arms and with her body. He jerked once more, then arched his back, spilled himself inside her as his face twisted in agonized pleasure.

The arms that formed her prison gradually went lax. Too stunned to speak, Emma ducked around him, scooped her clothes off the floor, stepping into them as she moved, and headed for the house.

She was halfway up the path when she heard Seth's heavy footsteps behind her. She broke into a jog.

At the edge of the patio Mrs. Evans called to her. "Emma, dear. There you are."

Emma stopped in front of Seth's mother, breathing hard. Seth stepped in place behind her. She didn't look back.

"Do you know what time it is? We have a million things to do before the ceremony," Mrs. Evans chided, hooking Emma's elbow and tugging her away and picking at the tangled mop on Emma's head with her free hand. "Starting with fixing your hair."

Emma obediently followed her future mother-in-law into the house. If Mrs. Evans noticed Emma was still wearing last night's evening clothes well after 8:00 a.m., or smelled the sex on her, she was too polite to mention it.

A cocktail in one hand, Seth tugged at the collar of his tuxedo with the other and struggled to remember his script. "Yes, the break-in was serious stuff," he told the man whose name he didn't remember, but whose face he recognized as belonging to one of several friendly, small-time competitors for yacht sales in the Emerald Cove area. The man didn't look like a traitor, with a beer belly lapping over his belt and a used-car-salesman smile, but then, what was a yellow-bellied turncoat supposed to look like?

In all probability, the traitor was a navy man, but inviting Seth's clients, co-workers, hell, half of Emerald Cove to the wedding covered two bases. One, it created a crowd, which should give the traitor a sense of anonymity. The feeling he could blend in, disappear.

He wouldn't know the cameras would be watching every move.

Two, if they were wrong about the traitor being military, it gave the villain a free pass onto the Evans estate. A chance at Stingray.

Until someone revealed himself as the man selling out Stingray, Seth planted misinformation in every ear he could bend. Just in case. "Not to worry, though," he told one of his top clients from St. Petersburg. "I've moved everything that's worth anything to someplace safe while I revamp building security downtown. All my secrets are safe. I guarantee it."

He clapped the man on the back and moved on to his next mark. Waiting for a clique of local business owners to break up so that he could get a word in with Mark Boorman, the president of the Emerald Cove Chamber of Commerce, he glanced at his parents' house. Automatically his eyes zoomed in on the second floor, where Emma had disappeared an hour before guests started arriving. She hadn't come down yet, as far as he knew.

A part of him wanted to forget the guests, the mission, Stingray, and go to her. Was she sick again? Or just mad?

She had every right to be either. He was feeling decidedly queasy himself. He'd wanted to tell her he loved her with pretty words and tender touches. Instead he'd colored the moment with ugliness.

Maybe she was right. Maybe he was afraid. Maybe on some subconscious level he'd wanted to drive her away.

He turned to go to her, got in two steps toward the house before a hand clamped over his shoulder. Without a word, Marcus pointed him at Boorman, who now stood alone, reminding Seth of his purpose.

Sucking in a bolstering breath, he stuck out his hand and strode forward. Emma would have to wait. "Mark, hey, good to see you. You heard about the excitement at my office, huh?"

Deep in the middle of lying to one of Emerald Cove's most upstanding businessmen, however, he found his attention drawn once again to the second floor windows.

Would she even come down for the ceremony?

He wouldn't blame her if she didn't.

Emma flipped the damp pillow over to the dry side and rubbed her cheek against smooth percale that still bore Seth's scent. She was wrinkling her spectacular ivory gown, messing the hair that Mrs. Evans's stylist had spent an hour coaxing to perfection and smearing her makeup, but she didn't care.

Just because she'd been lying in his bed for the last thirty minutes, crying into his pillow and inhaling his faint scent did not mean she loved him.

It definitely did not mean she was going to marry him. But she wasn't going to leave, either, no matter how desperately he tried to push her away. He was the one who told her to take what she wanted.

She wanted him.

The jerk.

She beat the feather pillow with her fist and burrowed her cheek into the down, but no more tears came. She'd cried herself out.

Reluctantly, she looked around the room Seth had grown up in—such a strange combination of a man's space and a boy's. There was a picture of him at about ten in a green and gold baseball uniform. He posed on one knee, grinning, with a ball and mitt held proudly before him. An electric razor on the built-in student desk. Advanced accounting textbooks sat on the same shelves as model airplanes and toy sailboats.

Pushing back the covers, she slid out of bed and went to study the personal odds and ends of Seth's life up close. A rumpled tablet sat catawampus on the corner of the desk. The tablet from the island. The one Seth had doodled in for hours on end.

She ran her fingers over the blank cover. His precious Stingray. She hadn't looked then. This time she didn't have the strength—or the desire—to resist.

Awe flooded her with warmth when she flipped open the cover. She'd had no idea he was such a talented artist, but he hadn't been designing submarines all those hours on the island.

He'd been sketching her.

Page after page of headshots, full body views, abstracts of just her eyes. He captured her serious side, her sense of humor, even her fear of the storm that had driven them together that last night. But each of the pictures had one thing in common.

Sensuality.

He captured an innate femininity in her. An ethereal, almost naive innocence in concert with a primitive carnality that she didn't see when she studied herself in the mirror but that stood out clearly in the images created by Seth's mind and hand.

Was this how he saw her? As some half-wild spirit creature in need of gentling? A fragile woman-child in a seductress's body?

Or did his emotions color his perceptions? Did his feelings for her filter the years, the experience, the mistakes from her features?

Was this how she looked through the eyes of love?

He'd said he loved her, and she hadn't even acknowledged the words. She'd run away from him, just as he'd predicted she would.

The need to find him, talk to him, touch him started as a low thrum in her core and pulsed outward. Her breath quickened with excitement. It wasn't too late for them. It couldn't be.

Straightening her rumpled gown, she headed for the adjoining bathroom to assess the damage to her makeup.

She'd just decided to wash her face and start over when she heard the voices.

"I'm telling you, Evans is a smart one," a husky voice whispered. "He wouldn't hide the Stingray files in his daddy's safe and then blab about it to everybody at the party. I'm betting they're up here somewhere. He'd want to keep them close. Like in his bedroom."

Stingray! The only people who even knew the project code name were Seth and his family, a few navy officials and Gideon Faulkner.

And the traitor.

Praying that neither squeaky hinges nor her hammering heart would give her away, Emma swung the bathroom door almost closed.

"You look through the desk," a higher-pitched but definitely still male voice squeaked. "I'll check under the pillow."

Emma angled herself for a better view through the slit between the door and the jamb, but the men weren't in her line of sight. Darn. If she could just get a look at them, the drama would all be over. They'd know who had broken into Evans Yachts, planted the bomb on the *Strictly Business,* run Seth down with a car.

"Aw, ain't this cute." The husky voice came from the vicinity of Seth's desk. "Lover boy's got a real hang-up for the blushing bride."

Soft footsteps padded across the carpet, then a low whistle broke the silence. "She's a real piece," the squeaky voice said. "No wonder he's in such a rush to get hitched."

"He's in a hurry because she's already knocked up, moron."

Emma heard paper crumpling, and oddly, her chest tightened more from the knowledge they were destroying one of his beautiful drawings than in reaction to the crude comment.

"Get back to work, and be quick about it," the husky-voiced man ordered. "You think we got all day before someone finds us?"

"Aw, we'll just say we was looking for the can."

"Yeah, that'll work. We only passed about six of them on the way up here."

For the next few minutes, Emma heard them searching the room. She tried several times, but she couldn't get a look at them.

Then even the minimal noises of their search stopped cold.

Voices and footsteps moved down the hallway, past Seth's now-silent room.

"That was close," the husky voice said when the passersby were gone.

"Let's get out of here," the other man replied. "We ain't gonna find nothing."

"Wait. Check the bathroom first."

Emma's blood ran cold. There was no exit from the bathroom other than the door into Seth's room. The window was too small, and she was on the second story.

The shower stall. Beveled glass distorted the view of the interior. If she lay down on the floor and held very still, maybe they wouldn't see her.

She stepped inside and was pulling the door gently shut when her elbow knocked a back scrubber off a ledge. The thud the soft rubber made when it connected with the ceramic tile floor sounded like a cannon shot to Emma, but it couldn't really have been that loud, could it?

The men were arguing about who should search the bathroom and who should stand lookout. When they didn't come rushing in to check out the noise, she assumed they hadn't heard. Actually, she fervently prayed they hadn't heard.

Her prayers were answered.

"We ain't gonna find nothing," the squeaky-voiced one said. "Why risk getting caught up here?"

The other man huffed out his annoyance, but capitulated. "All right, let's go. You first, and don't make no noise."

To Emma's great relief, she heard them shuffle to the hallway, then close Seth's door behind them.

She counted to one hundred, then counted to one hundred again to be sure they were gone, before easing the bathroom door open and slipping out.

"Gotcha!"

Something heavy and fuzzy dropped over her head and encased her like a shroud. She tried to scream but the husky guy had hooked a meaty arm over her face and mouth. He pushed her to the floor, and with his weight on her chest, she couldn't draw enough air to gasp, much less scream.

She kicked with all her might. Clawed for air, for light.

"Get her legs!" her captor ordered. "Get her arms."

"I've got a better idea," the squeaky-voiced one said. "Keep still, bitch, or I'll have to hurt you."

Emma heard a click, and something cold and sharp pricked her left side, low, near her belly.

Her baby! No. Oh, God, please not her baby.

She gave up her struggle. Let them do what they wanted, as long as they didn't hurt her baby.

"Now we got her, what're we gonna do with her?" the knife-wielding man asked.

"You kidding? We got us a goldmine here. Judging by them pictures, Evans would give anything to get her back. We're going to trade her, that's what we're going to do. Trade her for Stingray."

"How're we going to get her out of here?"

"Go downstairs, get that big ice box out of the back of the truck. Meet me at the bottom of the back stairs."

"What if she screams?"

"She won't."

Grunting, the beefy one shifted his weight off her. Something heavy scraped across the tabletop above her.

When the knife left her side, she opened her mouth to yell, to call for Seth.

Then her head exploded, and she wasn't capable of calling anyone.

Sixteen

The guests had gathered in the garden, where rows of rented white chairs rippled out from the lily-draped gazebo in concentric semicircles. The caterers were almost out of caviar canapés and the minister was checking his watch every few seconds when Seth went off in search of his bride-to-be.

The kitchen was empty save for a few uniformed servers refilling food trays. The parlor and living room stood silent.

She had to be upstairs.

The dress she'd worn last night lay rumpled on the bed in the guest room she'd been occupying, but Emma was nowhere in sight.

Seth knocked three times on the door at the end of the hall before entering. Holt sat with his feet propped on the table, staring at the fuzzy black-and-white security monitors displaying their father's empty office and the interior of the *Pisces*. Marcus's wife, Samantha, sat next to him, holding her sleeping infant son against her chest. She'd flown in last night for the wedding, but Marcus wouldn't let her mingle when he wasn't there to hover over her and their son. Said he couldn't afford the distraction with a traitor about.

Seth could understand that. He was beginning to understand a lot about protectiveness. ''You seen Emma anywhere?''

"Not for a couple of hours. Why? Afraid she's going to leave you standing at the altar?"

Holt's smile fell as he looked over his shoulder at Seth. He dropped his feet to the floor. "Hey, something wrong?"

"I don't know," Seth said, already on his way out. He pointed back at the monitors. "Keep your eye on the ball."

Seth strode over the plush hallway carpet with no clear idea where he was going. Where was Emma? Had she left as he'd asked?

He didn't kid himself. If she'd left, it wasn't because he'd asked. And it wasn't for a short visit with her family.

She wasn't coming back.

He almost laughed at the irony. In the emotional storm of admitting that he loved her, and was afraid of losing her, he may have caused exactly that to happen. A self-fulfilling prophecy.

God, Emma. Where are you?

He passed by his room, stopped. The door was cracked open. He was sure he'd left it closed. With one palm he pushed it wide. "Emma?"

No answer.

The short hairs on his forearms and the back of his neck prickled. *Trouble.* He could feel it.

Cautiously, he stepped over the threshold. At first glance, all appeared well. Then he noticed the drawing tablet he was sure he'd left closed laying open on his desk, one of his pencil sketches of Emma smiling up at him. The hand-woven blanket his half-Seminole grandmother had given him was missing from its rack at the end of his bed. The ceramic lamp from his nightstand lay on the floor, partially under the bed.

He crouched next to the fallen lamp, fingered a small red stain on the carpet.

Blood.

"Emma!"

He thundered down the hallway. Holt poked his head out of the monitor room, a worried frown ruining his beach-boy smile.

"Find Marcus and Drew," Seth ordered without slowing. "Someone's got Emma."

He took the stairs four at a time. Outside, guests stared at him curiously as he shoved through the crowd toward the driveway. The gates were closed. Holt would have told him if anyone had gone in or out.

He ran to the side entrance. Two catering trucks sat parked near the door. Jean-Pierre, the pastry chef, leaned on the bumper of one, smoking a cigarette.

"Did you see anyone out here? Emma?"

Jean-Pierre crushed out his smoke. "No, *monsieur.* Is everything all right?"

Seth didn't have time to answer. His eyes narrowed on a pair of white-jacketed figures toting a large, heavy white box onto the docks. He nodded toward the men. "Those guys work for you?"

Jean-Pierre squinted. "No. No, I do not think so."

Seth hesitated only a moment, puzzling it out. If someone wanted to smuggle a body—God, no. He wouldn't let himself think that way. They wouldn't bother to remove the body if she was dead. Smuggle a *person,* out of the house, a catering box would do the trick. But with Jean-Pierre taking a break by his trucks, they wouldn't have been able to load her up and drive her off. That would leave only one way to get her off the grounds—the docks.

Ignoring the pain, Seth hit the path to the water like

an Olympic sprinter. A quarter of the way there, he
saw the two Seadoos fifty yards down shore from the
docks, and cursed when the guys in white jackets saw
them, too.

The *Pisces* wasn't a problem. She was locked up
tight, her gas tank drained. Seth hadn't wanted someone to make off with his father's yacht because the
Stingray plans were supposedly aboard. Holt's new
race boat didn't concern him. The sleek sixty-footer
was fast, but even under ideal wind conditions, a sail-
boat would make a cumbersome escape vehicle, and
today's wispy breeze could hardly be called ideal.

But those Seadoos. He hadn't thought about them.
Hadn't considered them a threat.

The phony caterers set down their box, opened the
lid and lifted out a lumpy bundle. A lumpy, squirming
bundle the same color orange as the wool blanket
missing from his bedroom.

"Emma!" His lungs burned. His throat constricted.
His feet pumped harder in the sand.

The men looked back at him, but they were too far
away for Seth to make out their faces. One was heavier, gray-haired maybe. The other tall and thin. They
half carried, half dragged their bundle toward the Seadoos.

Seth veered away from the docks, but realized the
error of the choice as he tripped over a razor-sharp
clump of saw grass. He stood, watched the men zoom
away from the private marina, Emma balanced across
the seat in front of the heavier man. In minutes they'd
hit open water and he'd lose them.

He turned back to the docks and ran again, limping
noticeably this time. At the floating building attached
to the last pier, he fished a key out of his pocket and

opened the padlock on the door of the damp, cool boathouse. Jumping into his ace in the hole, his secret weapon, he slapped a kiss onto the windshield of the *Purely Pleasure*. "I'm going to need everything you've got baby, and no time to warm up."

The twenty-eight foot cigarette-style boat's twin 496/350 Mercruiser engines fired up with a throaty roar. Seth eased the throttle forward and nosed her into the sun, her red glittery bow sparkling. Bracing himself, he threw her wide open, and even expecting the burst of speed she gave him, he nearly lost his footing.

He scanned the horizon for the Seadoos, nearly panicking when he couldn't find them, then swallowing a lobster-size lump of relief when he spotted the lime green watercraft bouncing across the surf at two o'clock.

He bore down on them at a speed well past pleasure boating guidelines and into the professional racing range. Spray crested over the bow and hit his face like tiny darts. Wind pulled at his cheeks. He nudged the throttle up another notch.

At four hundred yards, they saw him. At three hundred, they tried maneuvering. He followed smoothly. At two hundred yards, they panicked.

The heavier rider spun his Seadoo in a tight spiral and stopped. Though Seth wasn't close enough to see his eyes, he was sure the man was looking right at him. Challenging.

He pushed Emma into the water, then whooshed off to catch his buddy.

"No." Seth pushed the throttle as far forward as it would go. The wind whipped tears into his eyes. His only excuse for the tears in his throat was what he'd seen. What his mind saw. Emma trussed and sinking.

Drowning.

"Damn it. No!"

The kidnappers forgotten, Seth kept his eye on the patch of ocean where he'd last seen Emma. Unwilling to lose even a second in getting to her, he pushed the boat at top speed all the way to the spot, then cut the engines and cursed the precious seconds he lost slowing the boat so he could jump overboard. He wouldn't do Emma any good if he bailed too soon and broke his neck.

Even at the lower speed the water felt more like concrete when he dove in. His momentum carried him across the surface like a skipping stone before he broke through. Sunlight dimmed to murk. An ominous silence surrounded him, broken only by the chugging beat of his heart and the gurgle of the current. Searching the dark vastness beneath him, Seth felt as if he was eerily reliving the scene from four weeks ago, when the *Strictly Business* sank.

He'd found her in time then. He'd find her this time, too.

Please, God, let him find her.

As if by command an orange cloud floated into his peripheral vision like a piece of overgrown plankton. Lungs about to explode, he stroked toward it, grabbed it, kicked toward the surface.

His heart kick-started when he felt movement inside the blanket. Putting all his might, all his will into it, he ripped at the bindings—cords from his mother's draperies—trapping her inside the wet wool. When he finally had her free and she coughed and sputtered and kissed him with her blue lips and wrapped her shaking arms around his neck, he finally remembered to breathe.

And to thank God.

Emma sat under a mountain of blankets in the center of Seth's big bed, warming her hands on a steaming mug of tea.

The mattress squeaked as Seth leaned over her for the thousandth time. "You sure you don't want to go to the hospital?"

"I'm okay." She worked up a passable smile. "Even the paramedics said so."

He reached out and touched her hair, and the worry he transmitted in the simple gesture made her heart ache. "So call me a worrywart. That's twice you've nearly drowned on me, Emma. You keep this up, I'm going to have to have a pair of water wings permanently attached to you."

She pulled her lower lip between her teeth, tried to suppress her giggle, but couldn't quite hold it back. He cupped her chin, turned her head up.

Molten regret swirled in his golden eyes. "I'm sorry, Emma. I'm sorry for getting you involved in this. Sorry for ever doubting that you would do the right thing when it came to the baby. But most of all, I'm sorry about this morning."

"Let's not talk about it, okay?"

She ducked out of his hand. He reached out as if to make her look at him again, then closed his fingers to a fist. Instead of forcing her, he slid off the bed, knelt beside her where he could look up at her. He set her cup aside and folded her hands in his, as if in prayer.

"I need to talk about it. You were right. You scared me." He sounded as if he'd swallowed a load of gravel. "I fell in love with you, and I didn't know what to do about it. All these years I thought I could never trust a woman again. Turns out it was myself I didn't trust. I didn't think I was capable of love anymore. I'm still not sure. But I know I want to try. Because I realized when I saw you go off that Seadoo and underwater that nothing scares me more than the thought of losing you."

Awe took away the chill the sea had put in her bones. "I trust you," she said.

He squeezed her hand. "Do you trust me enough to believe that you'll never be excess baggage in my life? Never a burden? That you *are* my life?"

Her heartstrings strummed an aching tune. So many insecurities between them, she thought. So much pain.

"I'm not sure," she answered truthfully. He looked away, but she drew his gaze back with a hand squeeze of her own. "But I want to try."

He smiled tentatively. "Maybe we could try together."

"Maybe."

An awkward silence spanned the remaining gulf left between them. They both wanted to try, but neither knew where to start.

"I talked to the minister before he left," Seth finally offered softly. "He said he could come back tomorrow evening. I'm not trying to force you here," he added quickly. "If you want to wait, I'm okay with that. I trust you, too."

Emma's heart stuttered. "Tomorrow evening?"

He hitched up one corner of his mouth. "I would have tried for the morning, but if today was any indication…well, it tends to ruin the wedding photos when the bride can't keep her breakfast down."

She punched him in the arm.

"Ow."

"Just for that, I'm going to make you ask me properly."

"I'm already on my knees. I don't know how to be any more proper."

"You can say the words. Nicely."

He straightened his back, squared his shoulders.

The valiant prince bent to one knee before her, his back straight, his shoulders square. "I love you, Emma Carpenter," he said, his voice true and clear. "I promise to love you and cherish you for the rest of our days. Will you marry me?"

Emma blinked as the daydream faded. The prince's face morphed, dissolved into Seth's. She had a feeling her prince and her pirate captain, not to mention Agent Omega, wouldn't be back for a while. She hadn't been looking for action and adventure in her daydreams all these years, she realized.

She'd been looking for a hero.

Now that she'd found him, she could put her imagination to rest.

"Emma? Emma, you're scaring me again. Are you going to answer me, or just leave me to a slow, agonizing death of wondering?"

She flung her arms around his neck. "Yes. Yes, I'll marry you. Today, tomorrow or any day you want."

The sun setting over the bride and groom's shoulders cast the cove in glittering bronze. Minister Parker gazed benevolently down on Emma and Seth, then out at the witnesses. This time they'd limited the guests to a small cluster of close friends and family, including Drew and Marcus's younger sister, Honey Evans Strong, and her husband Max, who might be the only two people happy about the one-day delay. They'd been out of the country when they got word about the wedding, and weren't able to get back until this morning. Having Honey here made it seem even more odd that Marcus and Drew were missing. They doted on their baby sister.

Emma knew Marcus had flown to Washington this morning to debrief the brass on the attempted kidnapping, but he should have been back in time for the ceremony. His absence didn't bode well for the future of Evans Yachts in the Stingray project, or for Emma's standing with the navy, but they'd finally decided to start the wedding without him.

Emma's standing with the navy didn't mean as much to her as it once had, as long as they didn't try to throw her in Leavenworth. She didn't think she was cut out to be a spy. Besides, espionage and motherhood didn't seem like a likely combination, and she'd had quite enough excitement and adventure for one lifetime. She was looking forward to full-time mommyhood now, maybe with a little consulting for Seth's company on the side.

She planned to resign her commission.

Drew's absence from the nuptials was even more mysterious than Marcus's. When she asked Seth why his cousin hadn't shown up, Seth had said Drew would probably come by later. But he'd said it with a smile, so she didn't worry too much.

The ceremony was almost over before Emma could soak it all in—the beautiful dress she'd borrowed from Laura that shimmered like an iridescent clam shell when she moved, the sand between her bare toes, the heartfelt, loving look in her husband-to-be's eyes. She almost wanted to ask the minister to slow down, to give her time to memorize every detail before he nodded for her and Seth to exchange rings and say the simple vows they'd written for each other. Almost.

She slipped the groom's ring on Seth's finger first. "Today and all my tomorrows belong to you. With this ring, I give you myself, and my promise of forever."

His eyes reflected his understanding of her message. She would never leave him. Breaking with tradition, he bent and kissed her lightly on the cheek before placing his ring on her finger. "In the ring of my love," he said, his warm gaze melting a hole in her, "you are the center."

If she'd been any happier with his message to her, her knees would have buckled from joy.

The minister had just begun to pronounce them man and wife when a pair of dolphins arced out of the water. Seth and Emma's indrawn breaths, along with the *oohs* and *ahhs* of the family behind them, made him pause.

The dolphins, a mating pair, curved gracefully through the air, then splashed down and leaped repeatedly. The larger of the two jumped straight up, waggling his tail as if dancing on the water. Then they dove, not to be seen again.

"You may now kiss the bride," Minister Parker said, and closed his bible.

Seth stared at the spot where the dolphins had disappeared as if transfixed. After a moment, Emma elbowed him. He turned to her, and his glazed eyes quickly focused. His lips met hers warmly, securely. More promise than kiss.

Before she could make a promise of her own, a downpour of birdseed rained over her and Seth. The Evans family swept its newest couple toward the house like the lead float in a homecoming parade. Halfway up the path, though, Seth turned her toward the docks. Surprisingly, the family kept going, as if they'd expected to leave the bride and groom behind.

Or maybe not so surprisingly. She narrowed her eyes at Seth. "What are you up to?"

He lifted his brows in an innocent "Who, me?" expression. Luckily for him, Marcus appeared on the path to the docks before she had a chance to torture an explanation out of her new husband.

Husband. She liked the sound of that.

"You're off the hook," Marcus said to Emma when he reached them. "Your human submersible act convinced the brass that you weren't part of the plot to steal Stingray."

Seth's shoulders relaxed. Partially. "What about the contract?"

Marcus jerked his head sideways. "They're worried about security, but mostly they don't think you've made enough progress on the speed issue. I'm sorry."

A muscle ticked in Seth's jaw. The wrinkles around his eyes tightened. "Got a pen?" he asked Marcus.

Marcus dug a ballpoint out of his pocket.

"Paper?"

He found a travel itinerary. The back was blank.

Seth made a spinning motion with his finger. Emma turned around and he smoothed the paper across her shoulders. For what seemed like an eternity, the pen danced across her back in quick shuffles and long dips. Finally Seth handed paper and the pen to Marcus. "You give that to the navy engineers."

Marcus scanned the notes, brow furrowed. "Is that—"

"Yes."

"Whoa. I don't think you're going to have to worry about that contract."

"Give a copy to Gideon, too. Ask him to see what he can do with it until I get back."

"What—" Emma started, then looked at Seth. "Until you get back from where?"

As if on cue, Drew's seaplane banked in from open water. Slack-jawed, Emma watched as he touched down in the cove and taxied up the canal to the Evans dock.

"You go," Marcus told Seth, and waved the folded paper in a shooing motion. "Do the honeymoon thing. I'll take care of the navy."

Emma looked from one Evans to the other. *"Honeymoon?"*

Hours later, Emma lay on a fresh pallet of palm fronds and ferns, Seth's arms around her, her sated body gilded in the last dying flickers of the single candle still burning. The other two dozen or so that had been lit when Seth led her into "their" hut on "their" island had burned down to nothing.

Emma felt a special kinship with them. She wasn't too far removed from a puddle of warm wax herself.

Still, a modicum of practicality settled in one of the three functioning brain cells she had left. The rest had shorted out in the last bout of lovemaking. "Do you think it's safe to stay here?"

They hadn't caught the men who had kidnapped her. Hadn't even gotten a good enough look at them to give a description to the police.

Seth pointed one long finger at the gym bag he'd left by the door. "I've got a flare gun and a radio. And

Holt has the *Pisces* anchored just around the point in case we need him.''

She snuggled deeper into his embrace, reassured as much by his strong body next to her as by the preparations he'd made, and yawned. "What was all that 'Whoa' and 'give this to Gideon' stuff with Marcus?"

He propped himself up on one elbow, excitement glittering in his eyes. "Did you see the dolphins during the ceremony?"

"Of course. Weren't they beautiful?"

"Did you see how they move?" He waggled his hand like a swimming fish. "Fast. Almost silent."

Her eyelids wanted to drift shut. "You're going to use dolphins to pull your submarine?"

He laughed. "I'm going to use a flexible tail to push it. Like the dolphins push themselves through the water. Like a swimmer's kick, it'll give just enough extra oomph to the engines to get the speed I need. It came to me while I was watching the dolphins. I read about similar research they'd done at University of California at Berkley awhile back, but I'd forgotten it." He started imitating fish with his hand again, talking faster. "I only need a couple of degrees of flex. I'll build in vacuums and pumps to get the swish effect, use the ballast—"

Sloughing off her drowsiness she turned to face him and placed a finger over his lips. "You were designing a submarine during our wedding ceremony?"

He shrugged sheepishly and kissed her fingertip. "Just for a minute."

"So you're really going to build Stingray."

"Yeah. I am."

"Even though someone is willing to kill you for it."

"I think we scared them pretty good today. They don't know for sure if we got a look at them, know who they are. They'll back off."

"For a while."

He gathered her up, sighed in her ear. "Do you want me to quit the project? I will."

Burrowing her cheek against his shoulder, she bit her lip. She'd spent too long in the navy to like the idea of abandoning a project this important to her country's defense. "No. I just want you to be careful. I—" She took his hand and put it over their son or daughter. "*We* need you."

"Nothing's going to happen to any of us. I swear it." He pulled his head back. "We'll take care of each other. We're together in this, right?"

"Right."

"I love you, Emma." His hands moving over her knowingly.

She arched against the familiar contour of his hard body. "I love you."

The last candle sputtered out, but Emma didn't mind.

The light of their love was strong enough to shine through any darkness.

* * * * *

Don't miss the next exciting title in the
FAMILY SECRETS *series,*
UNCHARTED WATERS by Linda Castillo
FAMILY SECRETS: *In Emerald Cove, blood*
is thicker than water.

Where love comes alive™

From first love to forever, these love stories are
for today's woman with traditional values.

Silhouette® Desire®

A highly passionate, emotionally powerful
and always provocative read.

Silhouette®

SPECIAL EDITION™

Emotional, compelling stories that capture the
intensity of living, loving and creating a family in
today's world.

Silhouette®

INTIMATE MOMENTS™

A roller-coaster read that delivers romantic thrills
in a world of suspense, adventure and more.

Visit Silhouette at www.eHarlequin.com

SDIR2